Eddie's Diner

By JD Cooper

Other books by the author

A Cup of Tea with Mr Johnstone

Dorcas the Invisible Cleaner

The Orb of Alberston

'You only know me as you see me, not as I actually am' – Immanuel Kant

'And those who were seen dancing were thought to be insane by those who could not hear the music' – Friedrich Nietzsche

'My advice is to never do tomorrow what you can do today; procrastination is the thief of time' – Charles Dickens

Table of Contents

Prologue

Here I am again, outside the 'headmasters' study', sitting in a hallway, wooden panelled walls lined with pictures of my colleagues, past and present - all dressed in corporate suits, all smiling that corporate smile. All facing the same way, right profile to camera…chin up….and…. say gorgonzola.

Me though? I don't appear on the walls at the moment, I am in disgrace. I have fallen foul of The Panel.

I have had the temerity to 'think outside the box' if one were being positive about it - I have had the audacity to have 'gone rogue', if not.

I'm waiting to be 'offered guidance', to be offered a 'fresh start' - a 'new and exciting opportunity'.

I have to say though that the place has changed since I was last here…oh about two hundred years ago. The wooden panelled walls are a new touch - though sort of bringing a jaded grammar school feel to it all if I'm honest, and the ceiling tiles? One hundred and three obviously, though I couldn't tell you why, and there's always that one that has a brown stain on it, but only in the corner, and for no apparent reason.

I look at my hands and see that they are the hands of an ancient, an actual ancient. I wonder if the hands of any of The Panel are as ancient as mine, while I am in this form, and I severely doubt it. Oh yes, we all have to be in proper form when we are called to appear before The Panel - it's a very serious, very sombre business. On these occasions were one to dress up in their current guise…well - Alaska is the next place they would see that's all I am saying.

Alaska isn't a bad place I wouldn't have thought, lots of wide-open spaces, and I should know about those, I look after

Dakota for The Panel. So, the wide-open spaces wouldn't bother me - the cold…now the cold? Well, that would though. Dakota - one hundred degrees in the shade versus Alaska….probably minus something horrible in the shade.

Anyway, I am wondering, or is it wandering…The Panel…? What do they know? What do they actually know? I have been around for an awfully long time and they….well, they just haven't. The Panel itself has obviously, but these current incumbents? These recent additions to it? No. They are people brought in from other organisations to run this one, and what's their experience in my field of expertise? Nothing, that's what. They may know how to manage, and that's still in dispute, but they are not workers, are not, actual, hands-on people. No, they will never get their hands dirty…..

"Etu? This way please"

A door opens, no-one opens it, it just opens. I am supposed to jump up now, I am supposed to walk in, with an apologetic look on my face and say how sorry I am, say that it won't happen again. Well, that's not happening, not today, not ever.

I stand. I pause. I sit again. I'm not playing their game. I will play mine. I will not be told what to do, not by these people, not by anyone. They have kept me waiting for too long - I will keep them waiting.

"Can you spell Montana, or how about Saskatchewan?"
"Coming…"

I stand. I pause and breathe deeply and then walk through the door. It swiftly closes behind me and I see The Panel, the current Panel for the first time in a long while. Their combined age is about a third of mine - what do they know?

They sit behind a huge mahogany desk, each with their corporate notepads, their corporate bottles of water, their corporate name plates in front of them, in case they forget who they are - I personally couldn't care less who they are though - they don't have my…..respect. Yes, that's the word - they don't have my respect.

"So, Etu. Why do you think you are here?"

I look around and see that there is a chair next to me. I am supposed to either ask to sit on it, or just sit on it - that's the first test. If I ask, then I am weak. If I sit without asking, then am I rude? And if I do sit on it, where it is, I am isolated - them behind their mahogany desk, and me, out in the open about ten feet away from them, where they can see me, examine me, see all my flinches and my wringing hands - that's what they would like. I pick up the chair, carry it about nine feet forwards and set it down again. No exposed NVC's here.

"I'm sorry. I wouldn't know, I've been a little busy recently as you are no doubt aware and haven't given it much thought to be honest" I replied.

"Then perhaps you should have done Etu - how about you take a moment now and have a think?"

"How about you just tell me? Then we can all get on with our day jobs"

"We appreciate that Dakota has been busier than usual for this time of year, but really, I would have thought that you would have planned for today?"

"Nope. Just bowled in. Rocked up. Sat outside for the best part of five years, in your newly refurbished corridor - very jaunty by the way"

"Yes. Sorry about that. We were just discussing what to do with you..."

"Shouldn't you have thought about that before now....you know, may be planned for it?"

"Careful Etu" advised one of The Panel members.

"Could I ask that we move things on a bit. As you said Dakota is very busy at the moment…and I can only juggle so many things while I am here? I do need to get back….this century if possible".

"Right. Very well then. We asked you to come here today as, even though Dakota is so very busy, and we do appreciate your efforts there, we feel that perhaps, it is possibly…well, that is to say.." one of them stammered and stumbled

"Time to move on Etu" another one didn't.

"Move on?" I asked "Move on to where? I am from Dakota. I am Dakota"

"Well. Your people…they….well…they"

"Careful…" it was my turn to advise the Panel members.

"They weren't always in Dakota though were they - they did move on didn't they - you know…..earlier, many years ago"

"I think what you are saying is, my *people*…..*my* people….were moved on…is I think what happened. And if you

7

are saying that…Let me ask you….are my figures good?"

"Yes"

"Are they just good, or are they very good?"

"They are very good Etu, we accept that….but…"

"Do I submit things on time? Do I always do what is asked?"

"Usually Etu. And that is why we asked you to come here".

"You didn't ask me to come here. You summoned me. You took me away from people who need me, from those who are even now in a state of limbo, and I would say abject distress, knowing the individuals as I do….for what? You could have emailed me - you could have called me and told me. Why make a performance of me having to come here at all?"

"You seem angry Etu?"

"Really? You keep using my name, so I will ask you. What are your names? Who are you people?"

"We are The Panel"

"I know what you are. That's what your name plate says. And yours. And yours. But what are your names - individually…who actually are you? That's what I'm asking"

"We are The Panel, and we ask the questions….Etu".

"Faceless"

"What?"

"Faceless is what I said… absolutely faceless".

"We are concerned about your figures, whilst good…"

"Very good"

"….very good, well….they could be better. Wouldn't you agree?"

"The figures could be higher, yes. I accept that"

"And yet they are not".

"No. The figures are 'very good' but could be higher….not better, just higher?"

"Exactly Etu, exactly".

"What about quality though? What about lasting quality? Do you ever think about the quality of what we do? Or is it more just about numbers".

"We have targets, the same as you Etu. We understand that".

"No. I don't think you do. Have any of you ever done my job?"

"Well, no, that isn't what we were brought in to do"

"So none of you know what it is like to look into the face of a dead person?"

"Well…no…that's not…."

"None of you have ever looked into that face, and seen the fear, the lost hope, the…the…desolation of a wasted life".

"Well, no….not exactly"

"You see when I look into a face - which I do, regularly, I have to make a decision. Me, no one else, not in Dakota anyway. I decide whether it is right or wrong to send that person back. Will they make amends, will they be a better person this time round? Or would it be better, kinder to let them go

- let them end their days and be remembered as the best they have been and accept it. Do you understand?"

"Well….yes….obviously….but that's not the point of this meeting…well it is…but"

"Look. Etu. The bottom line is you will do what you are told. Every time. The Panel is suffering, well, we all are suffering at the moment. Things are tight, financially, and getting worse, and we need every person to have a plan - every person - do you understand that?"

"It hasn't always been that way though has it?"

"Sorry?"

"I brought you people before - I brought you good people - people who were trying to make a difference and you turned me away. You let them die"

"That wasn't us. That was a former Panel, different times…now…we would urge you to sell everyone a plan, offer everyone a second opportunity".

"Regardless of if they are good or bad?"

"Well....no, not if..." said one Panel member.

"Everyone" said the one in the middle.

"What's the point?" I asked

"What?"

"What's the point? If I bring you everyone, you may as well give everyone eternal life and be done with it"

"Don't be ridiculous. Man cannot have eternal life".

"Me? Ridiculous? I'm not the one saying it doesn't matter how bad you are - you'll always get a second chance. And by the way I beg to differ. I know someone very close to me that has just that - that which man cannot have".

"Well, now, that was different... that was...."

"And why was that?"

"You don't need to know Etu. Decisions were made before us, above us and they don't concern you".

"But I am having to deal with it - with the fallout".

"That's the nature of the beast, I'm afraid. Look. What we are saying is that from now on, everyone, and we mean everyone gets a plan, gets a second chance".

"Because you need the money".

"Because we need the money. This organisation is not a charity Etu. It has to have money constantly coming into it. And for every person you turn down, making a unilateral decision, thinking you're doing the 'right thing' thinking you're somehow morally correct, well it has consequences….further along".

"Further up the food chain you mean - further up where bonuses are everything".

"Now. There is no need for that Etu. No need at all"

The Panel member - the one in the middle, the one who seemed to be in charge leant forward and passed me a piece of paper.

"What's this?" I asked.

"A written warning" they said.

"A written warning? After hundreds of years of work, good, decent, honest hard work….a written warning?"

"Read it again" they urged.

"A final written warning"

"A final written warning Etu. Any more of your 'thinking outside the box' any more of your independent views and Alaska will be like a balmy southern tropical holiday for you. Do you understand"?

I stood. I took the deepest breath I have ever taken in my long life. I had a decision to make…….

Chapter One

Tommy Zeitz - formerly Thomas Fitzroy Alexander Winstanley III was born, if not with a silver spoon in his mouth then not far short of it. His father, though he now publicly disowns him, was the renowned financier and overt fascist Thomas Winstanley II. His grandfather - the original Thomas Winstanley fought alongside his American brothers during two world wars whilst selling guns and other deadly weapons to the Germans and the Russians, making an absolute fortune in the process.

When the wars ended Thomas Winstanley made a generous donation to ensure the reconstruction of many buildings which were destroyed throughout Europe and instantly became famous for all his philanthropic works. He had however, the dubious habit of being extremely close to rivals who then mysteriously fell off cliffs, or under cars, or were shot by never identified snipers earning him the moniker of 'Lucky Tommy' - a name which he bore to the end when his son didn't fall off a cliff one day, preferring instead to encourage his father that it really was his turn.

Thomas Winstanley II also had numerous pieces of good fortune and in time successfully increased the family's wealth, so much so that Thomas Winstanley III became impatient and not having any actual work to do insisted that he had a football team bought for him to keep his interests away from cliff edges and so on.

Changing his name to Tommy Zeitz, for no other reason than there wasn't another Zeitz in pro football at the time, and to avoid any nepotism from his club owning father, Tommy landed at the Fighting Hawks training ground halfway through the season and informed them that he was their new quarterback. This came as somewhat of a surprise to the coach and to the current incumbent of that feted jersey. The Fighting Hawks then went from ten points clear at the top of their league to failing to make the playoffs and it was all thanks to the ineptitude of the new 'star' player Tommy Zeitz.

No one had heard of him, and with good reason - he had no form, no history - he had just turned up, donned a jersey, and not just any jersey, and said that he could play. The coach had tried speaking to the board, telling them they needed him gone, they needed the old quarterback to resume their previously winning season, but his efforts fell on deaf ears, or rather they didn't. They listened, they nodded, they 'uh uh'd' in all the right places, and then informed him the next day that he was fired.

Another coach came in and Tommy Zeitz continued as the starting quarterback.

The season was a failure and many of the players put in transfer requests, they knew what had happened, that money had spoken and that their careers would go the same way as the previous season if they stayed.

The following season however one teammate - now a second-string player decided that enough was enough. The new season had started badly - three losses on the spin and the papers talking about The Sinking Hawks, the Stinking Hawks and so on. Billy Jackson had had enough.

Billy had moved from quarterback into the defence and actually managed to do a decent job, but he still knew all the plays, he knew who went where and why, all he had to do was wait for his moment.

In the next game the Hawks were trailing twenty to nil in the second quarter, on their way to another humiliating loss when Billy saw the gap. There was a scrimmage, and the ball was snapped back to Tommy Zeitz, which was good in that the ball came to the quarterback, unfortunately for Tommy, Billy let his man through and as he ploughed into Tommy, Billy followed his man and the pair descended on top of the stunned quarterback. It was not only the ball that snapped that day - the crowd fell silent as they heard the crack of Tommy's neck, and as two players got up off the floor, Tommy's static body, twisted at an impossible angle, told the story of their landing.

Paramedics rushed onto the field, but it was obvious Tommy Zeitz would never play football again, although some would say he had never really played in the first place.

Tommy was taken to his father's own hospital, but it was later diagnosed that he would never walk again. His neck had been broken and the damage to his spine would make independent living an impossibility. Few people cried for Tommy, but his father knew what to do and made a call.

The candidates sit, nervously waiting in the hallway, side by side, each lost in their own thoughts, each in their own private worlds, clutching a leaflet, and each believing that they are the right one for the job.

A nervous Tommy Zeitz sits with the other candidates, clutching his leaflet - one which had been placed in his hand whilst a pillow was placed lightly, but firmly over his face, while he lay unable to protect himself in the hospital.

"Next. Actually, sorry. Thomas Winstanley please - is there a Thomas Winstanley".
"Yeh. Hi, that's me - well I'm actually Tommy Zeitz now".
"This way please Mr Winstanley"
"Its Zeitz - Tommy Zeitz"
"Not here it's not young man - come on through".

Tommy walked through the door, following a voice, as there was no one in front of him, and saw himself in a hospital bed, lying prostrate, currently with no pillow over his face, but still looking in bad shape.

"Hello Mr Winstanley. Do you know where you are?"

"In a hospital? I'm not stupid".

"Well, you're not, but you are - so one out of two. Would you accept that you cannot play pro football?"

"My father owns the team - it's my team, he bought it for me".

"Yes. To run, not to play. You cannot play pro football, please accept that".

"I will be the judge of that…"

"Then we will see you sooner than you think".

The candidates sit, nervously waiting in the hallway, side by side, each lost in their own thoughts, each in their own private worlds, clutching a leaflet, and each believing that they are the right one for the job.

This has been the way things have been done for years, for centuries in fact- and it is just the way things are. It is the way the world works. There are the people in charge, the people who make others wait, and then there are the waiters - the people who sit about and wait to be told what to do, where to go, who they are.

But there is one person who does not think he is the right one for the job, he does not believe it, he knows it - he knows he is the right man for the job - but he's not prepared to wait - to sit about wasting his time with all these others, these candidates - why should he wait - he is Tommy Zeitz and Tommy Zeitz doesn't wait for anyone.

A door at the end of the hallway opens, no one has opened it, it just opens, and a voice rings out.

"Next"

But before anyone else goes through the recently opened door, Tommy Zeitz goes through it. He breezes past all the waiters, all the candidates, for he is Tommy Zeitz and that means something - at least to him.

"Right. Me again" he says as he sits, in the locker room - the home team's, obviously.

"Ah. Mr Zeitz…how…pleasant to see you again? We were not expecting you so soon. What is it this time? Another injury? Another failed drug experiment? Another marriage hit the rocks?"

"Yeah. All of the above - anyway - I need to go round again".

"Don't we all Mr Zeitz, don't we all…but there is a limit, even for you - there are only so many years a person physically has in them".

"Do I need to speak to your boss…again. Look just show me the paperwork, I'll sign it and I'll be on my way".

"I wish you would…here".

"Whatever"

Tommy Zeitz - pro footballer, avid drug user and obnoxious man about town signs the reluctantly proffered paperwork and rising from his seat walks out of his former life and into his next one. He leaves the door open - he doesn't need to be civil; he doesn't need to show courtesy or respect to anyone - why....? Because he is Tommy Zeitz.

The Panel knew they had tried - they were being paid an awful lot of money, by an awful person, and had been for years and in return they had to keep Tommy going - had to keep giving him 'opportunities' as they were called.

You see The Panel ran Time, and over time, the organisation had become increasingly expensive - there were massive overheads and to keep things running they had had to call in a number of favours from numerous unsavoury characters, for whom in return, they ...well, they altered the rules a little.

Thomas Winstanley - the original one, had been one of those unsavoury characters, which probably should not come as a surprise - he had his fingers in all sorts of pies but had had no wish to continue past a certain age. If there was one good thing about Thomas Winstanley, and there weren't many things to choose from, it was that he knew when to move on. He had been offered the chance to go back and do good but had declined. He had been offered the 'opportunity' to alter his ways of old and had laughed - actually laughed at The Panel. 'Where would I be now', he had said, 'without my money. I had to do the things I did to get rich, and I was good at it. Why would I throw that all away?' he had said. It was quietly pointed out to him that he was currently dead as he had been gently nudged off the cliff - did Rock Falls ring a bell?

Now, Tommy Zeitz may have been stupid, and certainly thought that having miraculously recovered again and again from his injuries he could do anything. Having been let into the family secret this only enhanced his view that he was immortal.

Tommy left the Fighting Hawks by 'mutual consent' and next turned up at the Redrock Rollers - a team trying desperately to make their way into the elite game. But it was not to be, for them, or for Tommy as when he turned up and told the team that he owned them, the quarterback immediately put in a transfer request and Tommy quickly filled the gap.

In only their second game an old teammate of Tommy's suited up in the opposition changing room, not believing his luck. Billy Jackson took to the field with the biggest smile on his face. He was now five years older, and five years slower than he had once been, but this was still Tommy Zeitz and Tommy Zeitz was going down....again.

The Rollers were twenty to nil down in the second quarter when…..well you know the rest.

"Hello again Mr Winstanley…..just five years later then?"

"What the f…?"

"Sorry - you've still got some pillow - there - in the corner of your mouth…?"

"Who?"

"Your father, obviously - he's not a bad man really - he's trying to do you a favour I think".

"By killing me?"

"Only twice…..so far"

"Yeh, but even so…?"

"We have a proposition for you Tommy…?"

"Go on"

"Can we accept that pro football is a thing of the past?"

"OK….maybe…I'm not saying there won't be a comeback somewhere down the road, but maybe I'll rest up a while".

"Ah. Good. Progress. And could we ask that the alcohol, drugs, and the women be reduced….just a tadge?"

"Go on"

"Look, as you are aware your family has supported The Panel for many years now, and we are grateful….but you…well...you are a bit of a conundrum…"

"A thorn in our side" another voice shouted in Tommy's head.

"A pain in the ass" came another.

"Yes. Thank you. If we can remain professional please" the first voice requested - "We have a proposition for you. We want you to 'rest up' as you say, but somewhere specific, somewhere, out of the way, somewhere that you will not attract the…ah…attention that you do - you know media wise?"

"I like media attention - I am Tommy Zeitz after all".

"Yes. About that. The scandal last year - with those call girls, and the zebra….um - that sort of media attention surely is not good, even for you - certainly not for us, I'm sure you can see that?"

"Hey. All media attention is good media attention"

"No. No it's not. You are stupid aren't you?" said a second voice.

"A zebra…? I heard it was a….?" a third voice tried to interject.

"Again. Can we please remain professional - the specific type of animal is immaterial at this juncture. Mr Zeitz…Tommy….. What do you say? How about you rest up somewhere, out of the way, have a bit of fun…only a bit though…and then go to work for us? Sort of in an observational capacity?"

"What does that mean though".

"There is a man…well let's say…a man, calling himself Eddie, he runs a roadside eatery….a ….?"

"Diner? Why is that so hard for you to remember" a second voice prompted

"Yes. Thank you - a diner - nasty grubby establishment in …where was it?"
"Dakota" the second voice prompted again.
"Thank you. Dakota. And he is…well let's just say that he is not keeping in line with the aims and directions of the organisation. We need you to monitor him for us. Could you do that?"
"Sure"
"Without the booze, the drugs and the women?"
"Eventually….probably….
possibly….. hopefully"
"Good. Well, that's a start anyway. Now, do you have any questions?"
"What's in it for me?"
"Obviously…what would you like?"
"Eternal life" said Tommy.
"Eternal life?" choked the first voice.
"No…no…no"   spluttered the second voice.
"Absolutely not" said the third voice.
"How about I call my father and see what he suggests shall I?" Tommy queried of

The Panel. "See if there isn't another direction he can channel his money into - my money one day don't forget".

"Eternal life it is - sign here".

Chapter Two

The candidates sit, nervously waiting in the hallway, side by side, each lost in their own thoughts, each in their own private worlds, clutching a leaflet, and each believing that they are the right one for the job.

Some also believe that they have only just arrived, and have only been there a few minutes, if you look carefully you can see these ones - identify them as the new arrivals. They still pat their hair, brush lint off their immaculate suits, buff their shoes on the backs of their trousers. They still shuffle whatever paperwork they brought with them, on their laps - rehearsing their lines, practising their speeches.

Some who think they have arrived earlier than these newbies have already gone through that stage and now look around and at their watches, 'how much longer? How much longer?' they wonder.

Some who have actually been there much longer also look around, but more upwards at the ceiling, though it never changes no matter how long they look at it. They blow long and hard through their lips and count the ceiling tiles. Always one hundred and three, no matter which way they count them - why one hundred and three? And why an odd number?

The hallway is wide and long - wide enough for each candidate to see the person opposite them, but too long for them to see the start or end of the line.

Not even the shafts of dusty light coming from the ceiling windows allows the candidates to register the competition, to see the face of the person who may just beat them to the job. They have been told that there is not 'just one job' - that it hasn't been decided just how many positions are available.

They have been told that they are not in competition with each other - but that they are only in competition with one person, and that is themselves. Standard management speak , trying to put a person on edge, trying right from the start to put them on the back foot, and it often works.

A door at the end of the hallway opens, no one opened it, it just opens, and a voice rings out.

"Next"

Presumably someone goes through the open door as it closes and the candidates all shuffle one seat to the left.
This is it, they are getting closer, closer to the door, closer to their turn, or return, closer to their opportunity.

And   then   nothing.   Waiting.
Always waiting.

The door opens again.

"Next"

The door closes. Shuffle to the left.

Eventually Sarah is next to the door - she can see it clearly, its two hinges, its handle, brassy and shiny, and its keyhole. What would happen, she wonders, if she rose from her seat - oh so close to the door, and peeped through that keyhole - that portal to another world? It would only take a few seconds, and would anyone stop her, prevent her from looking into it?

She would ponder this time and again in the weeks to come but is, for the moment, interrupted in her thoughts.

"Next"

Sarah cannot move. She is, after all this time, stuck to her seat. She has been waiting so long, days she thinks, that she cannot free herself from the chair that has been hers for so long.

"Next. If it's not too much trouble?"

Wow ! A conversation, well, almost, with another person, well, not really, but at this point Sarah would take just about any contact, human or otherwise.
She rises from her position at the head of the queue and looks backwards.....there is no one else there.

Walking towards the open-door Sarah gets the sensation she has been here before and as she walks into the room beyond the door, through the portal she freezes. The room is her living room, in her house - the curtains drawn, just as they were when she had left them...this morning? Yesterday? A plate and a mug, half full of coffee - surely cold by now, still sit on the table where she had put them before she had left earlier. Why had she left so suddenly? She couldn't recall -

something   had   happened…?
Something….? To do with…?

"Please sit - Miss?" the voice invited her.
"….Sarah"
"Unusual surname"
"No. Sarah, it's my first name, my surname
is….? What is my surname? Sorry? I'm a
bit…? I've been waiting outside for…?
How long have I been waiting…?"
"Thirty minutes. You've been waiting
thirty of our minutes. We're sorry to have
kept you waiting for so long. It's normally
a quicker process than this, but your
predecessor…well…they …not so much
argued, as wanted to discuss the terms of
their….never mind. Tell us about
yourself…Miss?"
"Atkinson…I want to say Atkinson - Sarah
Atkinson…is that right?"
"It doesn't matter - let's just move
along…so, what can you tell us
about yourself?"

"Well, I'm thirty-three years old, married to Tony. We live in…..um….matrimony, happily….have done for some time…look, I'm sorry, can I start again? Can I go out and come in again - I'm nervous - I haven't been here before…"

"We would hope not. Alright. Listen. Sarah. Your age doesn't matter. Your marital status doesn't matter, and you may wish to think again on that subject. Where you lived doesn't matter, none of it matters. What matters is the future - your future and what you're going to do with it"

"I don't understand….my marital status..?"

"Focus. Please"

"Sorry"

"You have been chosen, identified if you will, to undergo a rigorous selection process for a very important position. Please don't make us think we've made a mistake, as we're not accustomed to making mistakes and we don't take kindly to those who make us make those mistakes. Do we make ourselves clear?"

"...Um....yes. Sorry"

"And stop apologising...."

"Yes. Sorry"

"So, Sarah. Do you understand the nature of the job you have applied for?"

"Um...yes....although I can't actually remember applying for it as such? But...well, I'm here now....so....yes...me...what can I tell you about me?"

"How about we take control of this situation shall we? The job for which there has been an application is a delicate one - we need someone who can deal with a difficult situation involving complicated people, or rather one particularly complicated person. Are you aware of Time?"

"Time?"

"Yes. Time. Are you aware of Time?"

"As a thing? Or as a concept? I'm sorry...what do you mean?"

"Time - for goodness' sake. It's quite clear isn't it. Do you understand Time"?

"Well, yes, but you're saying it like its someone, an actual person".

Another voice then spoke. It had not spoken before and, like the other voice - the one that had been speaking, it also, had no body attached to it. Both voices had just been in Sarah's head.

"Sarah. If I explain, but first a few questions if I may?"
"Certainly…Mr…?"
"Call me Terry - if that's easier?"
"Terry - OK, hello, please to meet you. Who was that other one - that other voice?"
"It doesn't matter - it's just you and I now."
"Yes. Just you and I"
"So, Time is a person. It is obviously also a thing - a concept as you rightly said. But in this instance, this particular instance it is a person. Their other name - their former name was Etu, but they go by another name at the moment - do you   know Dakota?"
"Dakota? North or South?"

"Um….? I don't know - does it matter?"

"I don't know either anyway, so no it probably doesn't".

"If you are accepted for this position you will need to go there, you don't have to know it as such, but just where it is - do you understand?"

"Yes. With you so far"

"Well having successfully arrived in North….or South Dakota, you will be tasked with a specific role for us - The Panel. Are you squeamish Sarah?"

"Squeamish?"

"You people really have the habit of repeating things don't you?"

"Do we…sorry - ah, I see what you mean. I'll just listen shall I?"

"Yes. If you wouldn't mind. There - in one of the Dakota's you will find a …a roadside….an eatery near the road…a…?"

"Diner?"

"Yes - that's it - a diner - it's called Eddie's Diner - nasty little grubby establishment, it's got a hotel thing attached to it…"

"It would be a motel I think, not a hotel…a hotel is…"

"If I may continue…?"

"Sorry".

"If selected…you will go there and seek out, and befriend a woman - a woman called Lorna…"

"How will I know her?"

"What?"

"How will I know her - what if I don't see her?"

"For goodness' sake, please listen. Lorna is there every day. She does not leave the place and you will need to encourage her to do so. Do you understand?"

"Yes….but why?"

"Now. That is going to be a problem if you ask why. As well as not liking to make mistakes, we do not like being questioned. We, The Panel, prefer, in fact, no, we demand that people we interact with, listen to us, and then carry out what we tell them to do. Would that be good for you Sarah?"

"Yes. I am sorry. I understand. Go to the diner…"

"Nasty grubby…."

"Establishment"

"Quite. And then….?"

"Befriend Lorna, get her to leave the diner…..and…?"

"Kill her"

"Sorry? And I mean - I beg your pardon…?"

"Kill her"

"I thought that's what you said…can I ask why?"

"No"

"Right….then …um if you don't mind…..can I withdraw my application please? This doesn't sound like the sort of thing I had in mind for career progression".

"No. You cannot …withdraw the application. You have been chosen…selected…and you will not question".

"Can I ask one question though please…?"

"One question"

"What would I get in return for carrying out this …..assignment?"

"Oh. Sorry…eternal life"

"Where do I sign?"

"Just here - and from now on you are Greta Johansson".

"Can I ask why?"

"No. That would be two questions".

Chapter Three

Hello Weary Traveller, and welcome to my world. I hope that you will feel comfortable while you're here, perhaps you'll stay a spell, and even accept it as I do, after all it's one we can't do a lot about now, we can only accept it, and maybe even enjoy it for what it is, or isn't.

I've been in this world for a fair time now and it hasn't been too bad to me, well not so far anyway. Oh, there have been times when I wish I was somewhere else, wished I was someone else, but, well, we can't all choose where we are, no more than we can choose who we are….but what if you could? Would you want that? Would you want to choose to be someone else, and to live their life? For a year? A month? Or even a day? Would you choose that? And if you did, then what would you give to have that?

I've had a few jobs in my time, and moved around a bit as they say. I've found it best to keep moving in my field. I nearly said profession then, but I wouldn't say that what I do is a profession as such, more of a past time, a leisure activity if you will - something to entertain myself in my latter years, and there have been so many of them.

I'm so old now and I can't really remember my younger years, they are too far behind me now to think about and what I do recall upsets me sometimes. It wasn't a happy time for me, but if we get along, I may tell you a little about then later, we'll see shall we? They say that talking things through with a stranger can help ease old wounds...well, we'll see - maybe we can swap our stories and help to ease each other's pain - who knows?

I've been around the block and have lived many lives and so I think I am pretty well placed to help others make their choices, or at least show them the options they have when they get to the position to make a choice - you see I always think that the ultimate choice, the final choice so to speak, has to be the individuals don't you? Oh, I could tell you what I think you should do, where I think you should go, who I think you should be even, but at the end of the day it is down to you. You are the one that has to live with the decision you make and so no one, not even me, should tell you what you should do, should they? It wouldn't be right. No, I would only be giving you my opinion, based on my experience obviously, but still my opinion only - it's not advice, you don't have to listen to me.

Oh, hold on a moment - there's a customer - I won't be a minute.

The bell rings above the old rickety door and as it opens a gale blows in, bringing with it the dust and dirt from the road outside. I've swept the forecourt of my motel so many times, but there really is no point - the debris just comes back to settle with me. I do it more for something to do, to pass the time between customers deciding to take a chance and spend some time at my establishment. I've no idea why they do it really, perhaps because it's the only motel in a hundred miles and is advertised as such. Who knows? A lot of potential customers choose not to believe the sign and drive straight past, continuing their journeys to who knows where? I wonder whether they arrive safely at their destinations, or like many decide that maybe they should turn back, you know, just in case the sign is right. The low-priced fuel at my garage, such as it is, is also possibly a draw to some as well - who knows the mind of the long-distance traveller, it's not the way I choose to pass my time.

Anyway, the bell rings and the door opens. The debris enters, as does a lone traveller - they're my favourite. Simple, straightforward, and usually easiest to please.

I don't mind families, honestly I don't, but they are harder to accommodate you see, harder to 'cater for' as we say in the trade. There's nothing for children to do here you see, no playground, no park, unless you count another load of sand and dirt out the back, but there's no swing, no slide - so no, children don't do well here. I can cater for families if I must, I can cook up some tasty treat in my little diner, but the menu is limited really to a few tried and tested dishes - hamburgers, chilli, even spaghetti, you know, that sort of thing - not exactly haut cuisine I'm sure you'll agree, but I try.

No. The single traveller is better all round - better for the person seeking a roof over their head and a bed for the night; and simpler for me…in case…. well - I'll come to that later. Let's see how we get on first.

Anyway, where were we - oh yes - the bell, the door, the debris - the lone traveller entering my motel.

"Good afternoon madam" I say to the woman as she removes her scarf from her head and slowly shakes her hair out from beneath it. It's strange that that always has a provocative and alluring effect to it in the movies, but here, in my now dusty reception, amongst the old magazines and noisy water cooler it doesn't. It is a practical act performed by someone who, well, just wants to shake the journey from their hair, nothing more.

"Hello" the woman says "I wondered if you had a room for the night, I'm passing through on my way to…"
"That's alright lady I don't need to know your life story - this is a business arrangement not an introduction service. You need a room, I have them, you can borrow one for as long as you wish, and

when you are ready you can settle up and continue on with your life. Does that seem in order?" I asked her.

"I am sorry. I didn't mean to …well to… I was just passing the time of day really…sorry" she stammered.

Oh God - clumsy me.

"No. I'm sorry. It is me who should apologise. I don't get that many customers through here this time of year and well, I sometimes forget how to interact with people - I'm a bit out of practice I suppose. I am sorry. Can we start again?" I offered.

"Certainly. Shall I go out and come in again?" the woman smiled.

"No. Let's just assume that you have…I'll go first again shall I? Good afternoon madam" I began again. I really must remember not to say the first thing that comes into my head. It's got me into a lot of trouble in the past and probably will in the future. I paused.

"Hello. I wondered if you had a room for the night please…I…" she also paused.

"Certainly madam, are you just passing through - on your way to somewhere else perhaps?" I smiled in return, nodding slightly to encourage her.

"I am. Yes. I am. I am on my way to Rock Falls. Do you know it?" she enquired

"Oh yes. Rock Falls, Colorado? - A lovely place I understand. I haven't been there myself, but they say the sights are lovely at this time of year. Absolutely lovely I'm told. I'm sure you'll enjoy it when you get there". This was more than I had said to one person in a week, and I was out of breath at the end of my motel receptionists' bit.

"Really?" the woman came back to me.

"Honestly? I've no idea. I'm just thinking about what a motel receptionist would say to engage with a customer. As I said I've not had a lot of practice recently you see. What takes you to Rock Falls? Business?

Pleasure? Sightseeing? Which is it?" I asked her.

"I'm throwing my husband off a cliff there" she stated bluntly.

"Oh?" I began "has he upset you in some way? Was he abusive to you? Mistreated you?"

"No. Not at all. He's not like that" the woman said.

"Was he unfaithful perhaps? I've never been married, so I don't know how these things work. It seems a bit extreme to throw someone off a cliff though - wouldn't divorce be, well tidier? Is he in the car at the moment? Does he know of your plans?" I had to know; she had intrigued me.

"Well, yes. He is in the car I suppose. Technically" the woman said.

"Oh, so a double room then, or would a twin be better? I have two singles if you'd prefer - you know, to avoid difficulties?"

"No. That's alright. He doesn't take up a lot of room. Just a single please - he will be staying in the car tonight" the woman stated quite matter-of-factly.

"Well. It's entirely up to you madam. Although there is a storm brewing. I'd hate for him to come to any harm - the winds do get up here you know" I informed her, just as the door conveniently rattled in its hinges as if to back me up.

The woman laughed, a pleasant laugh and it made me wonder what someone had done to cause this woman to take the action she intended tomorrow. It seemed very drastic, but who was I to judge people and cast blame in a relationship.

"It wouldn't take a lot to blow him away to be honest, not the state he's in at the moment. No, just a single please - that will be fine" the woman confirmed.

I nodded and handed the woman a registration card to complete - you know just the basics - name, home address, mobile, car plate number, and gave her a pen. As I handed it to her our hands briefly touched and I got such a jolt of electricity from this woman it was all I could do not to react and pull my hand back. I hadn't had such a jolt from a customer in many months, and it brought back a lot of feelings - both good, well quite good ones, and some very bad ones. I withdrew my hand and thought the woman had not noticed me react but then she said.

"Oh. Did you feel that - it was like a jolt of static? Did you feel it? It must be the carpet. Sorry"

"Yes. Perhaps. I keep meaning to get it changed - a few people have said the same thing. Sorry" I apologised.

"No. That's OK. Ooh. It quite woke me up. It's been a long drive so far and well, my husband, my soon to be ex-husband didn't exactly take his turn at the wheel. Do you do food here, and perhaps a beer? I'd murder a beer right now?" the woman asked.

I looked down at the registration card and said.

"Certainly. Mrs Greta Johansson of Illinois. Let me get your bags and then I'll show you to your room" I offered.

"You know that's not my real name, don't you?" the woman admitted.

"Why that name though? - Look, I really don't mind what you call yourself so long as you don't steal anything or break anything and provided you pay when you leave. I also take cash as I feel that helps people who need a motel in the middle of nowhere - don't you…..?"

"Sarah" the woman said.

"Sarah" I repeated "And the car outside bearing the New York plates is yours I presume?" I asked.

"Yes. That's mine. Well, it was my husband's …but…"

"He doesn't drive anymore?"

"Precisely….?" Sarah paused.

"Etu" I said.

"Etu?" the woman looked at me sideways.

"That used to be my name…Sarah - does it matter? - Call me Eddie if you prefer".

"Eddie. Pleased to meet you" Sarah said.

Chapter Four

I withdrew a room key from the board behind me - number six for Mrs Johansson from Illinois, I think, and having lifted the hatch to the reception desk I joined her in the foyer. When I say foyer I mean that little area between the desk and the door - that little bit that was now quite crowded, what with a customer and me in it. If truth be told it was me that made the place look crowded, but then again I made most places look crowded. I am just over six foot tall, even now, in my older years, and I am also, what is the polite term now, sturdy? Stocky? I'm not fat, no, no, I'm just solid. Sarah stood back against the wall to allow me to manoeuvre around her and out of the door and as she did, so she brushed up against the poster someone had put there some years before. It showed a happy smiling family out on a day trip. A family

58

fun day out? You know the sort, far too good-looking mum, dad and two children - all caught up in the moment, all fresh faced and smiling oh so naturally for the camera - terrible - not at all lifelike and in no way representational of the modern American family. Perhaps not surprising really as the date on the bottom of the poster was from about twenty years ago, I must swap it for something a little newer at some stage, you know, spruce the place up a bit.

Leading Sarah out onto the forecourt I pointed to her car.

"Shall I get your bags? Pop them in your room for you?" I offered.

"No, that's fine. I'll do it later; I tend to travel light. Can I get something to eat perhaps, and how about that beer?"

"Of course," I said, "please follow me" and led Sarah towards my little diner across from the motel.

The diner had seen better days, as had the motel to be honest, but I kept it all running as best I could. I was not what you would call an entrepreneur, more of a would-be businessman. I enjoy the idea of business, the thought that maybe one day I might be successful; but the practicalities, the actual work side of it eludes me, and I get easily distracted. Other things take over my mind and to be honest my interest. Even if I got this place up and running like a proper hotel complex, who would come? It's in the middle of nowhere for a good reason and off the beaten track to most, no, I like it the way it is, and the occasional lick of paint keeps it functional. It certainly is nothing spectacular, no Motel 6 or Super 8, but it is clean, and I've had no complaints from my guests, so it obviously does the job.

The diner has a large, seated area about the space of two reasonably sized train carriages side by side, with a kitchen and servery along one wall. It's nice, and I think it's very homely. When I'm here I enjoy the extra title of cook. I wouldn't call myself a chef, as I've said it's strictly standard fare, but people seem to accept it, they manage to keep it down, and that's all I can ask.

It's here though that I can introduce you to a member of my staff - she is my waitress - Lorna, and she is also my cousin of sorts, I'm told. I think a relative of mine knew a relative of hers at some point and so we think we are distantly related in some way. Lorna says she is twenty-three, but she acts about seventy-three sometimes. She is into all sorts of things, fast bikes, fast cars, and you guessed it - fast men. She's taking a breather though at the moment, away from her home life and currently resides, rent free in one of the rooms. I agreed with her mother to look after her for a bit until she gets herself straightened out - apparently the last fast man she was involved with had a slight accident with a fast car and it left Lorna a little upset - I think she truly loved that car.

Had she not been driving it at the time of the unfortunate event I am sure she would still be angry at the man concerned, who happened to be crossing the road on the way from her married sister's house in a state of undress. It was almost like she made a choice, the man or the car and the car won.

"Hello Eddie - got another lamb to the slaughter then?" Lorna called out from the waitress station at the end of the servery. Jumping down from her stool and standing at her full height of five feet two she smiled at Sarah. "Hello, please sit anywhere you like, I'll bring you a menu - did you want something to drink while chef fires up the microwave?"

"Thank you, that would be great, thank you - may I have a beer please - nothing non-alcoholic?" asked Sarah.

"Sure - coming right up. Take a seat" Lorna waved across the empty diner, indicating Sarah could sit anywhere she wished.

Sarah came fully into the diner and stopped when she saw the juke box - which is my pride and joy.

"Wow" she exclaimed "is that a Wurlitzer? It's fantastic"

"It's a Rock-Ola but nearly as good as a Wurlitzer, I think so anyway - have a go - see if there's anything you like. It's got all the usual standards - you know a few country, a few rock and roll, a lot of ballads, though we tend to keep it upbeat in here" I let Sarah know.

"23C !" Lorna called out "23C!"

Sarah approached the jukebox with what seemed like caution.

"I don't have any coins - do you have any change Eddie?" she asked.

"It's OK. It's free, I've sort of hooked it up so anyone can play whatever they want - though I'm thinking of putting a block on 23C - if I hear that tune again …" I told her.

Sara looked down at the songs and not being able to avoid it I saw her hand hover over 23C - The Shangri Las - Leader of the Pack.

"Don't do it Sarah. Anything else but that - please" I asked her.

I am a reasonable man all things considered, but I could not bear to hear that song again. Lorna felt it 'spoke to her', she felt it had 'an untold story to it" - though the story simply seemed to be a naive girl falls for a biker who decides to be too cocky and gets himself killed. I hadn't the heart to point out to Lorna that her story was that of a naive young girl who falls for an older, and as it turned out married man, who decides to get caught with her sister in a compromising position and upon leaving via the bedroom window gets mowed down by the now, not naive girl in a speeding car - hardly similar. I've checked that jukebox and there isn't a song to cover those circumstances, and nor should there be.

Sarah chose common sense and went for a country ballad - but again it was something about a man leaving his woman for another though it pained him, and something about having to shoot his horse, or dog - I wasn't really listening. Christ help us - give me Led Zep any time.

Whilst I stood at the freezer thinking what culinary delights I could tempt Sarah with, Lorna walked over to her with a Corona on a silver tray - a silver tray no less, now that's class !

"Here you are. Try that. Have you had a chance to look at the extensive menu of this fine eatery madam?"

"Er, yes - is there something you can recommend perhaps?"

"Yeh - phone for a take-out is my advice".

"Lorna !" I called over "Give the lady the choices and let her decide".

"Yeah, yeah Eddie - I hear you" Lorna replied.

"I'll take the hamburger and maybe some fries, and some slaw, if that's OK?"

"Coming right up" Lorna stepped away from the table and called "number three Eddie with slaw" and resumed her usual spot at the end of the servery.

A short time later I slid a wonderfully prepared hamburger and fries with a tub of slaw on the side down the counter to the waiting Lorna. She stood and, wiping the tray from earlier, placed the plate lovingly on it before carrying it over to Sarah and setting it before her.

"Another beer?" she asked.

"Oh yes. Keep them coming, Lorna. Thanks" Sarah replied.

There were no other customers in the diner that afternoon and so service was swift and after only a few songs and a few beers

Sarah said she would retire for the night. It was just about sunset and apart from any late-night stragglers I doubted we would get any more customers in tonight. I told Lorna she could wash up and then lock up and I would go back to the reception to do the same.

Walking back to the rooms with Sarah I felt she might stay a little longer than the passing through she initially had said - we would see in the morning.

As we came to the rooms - about twenty of them all told Sarah stopped and turned towards me.

"Who do those cars belong to Eddie? Are they yours?" she asked as she pointed through a walkway between two rooms?

"Oh no," I said, "they belong to the other guests. We get a few people from time to time who stay here a while, sort of rest up, before going on with their journey. The longer-term ones put their cars out back or ask us to if they are busy - you know, sort of a valet service".

"Oh, I see - how very up market" Sarah smiled at me "Goodnight Eddie - thanks for the burger - it was actually quite nice".

"Thank you Sarah - I am glad you enjoyed it - see you in the morning. We have breakfast between eight and ten?" I advised her.

"OK thanks Eddie - good night" she said.

"Good night" I said and walked towards the reception.

I sat back behind my hatch, put my large feet up on the counter and pulled out the registration card Sarah had filled in. Mrs Greta Johansson indeed - why that name though I thought, why make up a name out of thin air. I couldn't care less if she was a Sarah or a Greta - that sort of detail didn't matter here, and certainly didn't matter if Sarah wanted to go back - or perhaps it did. Perhaps the name was based on a reality -

something that meant something to her? Had meant something to her?

Chapter Five

I don't sleep anymore; I haven't done so for a while now. I can't seem to totally rest and the thought of me being unconscious whilst others are walking around doing goodness knows what, is quite frankly frightening to me. I don't like being out of control or letting others be too much in control. I have my position to think of, being the manager and owner here obviously, but a lot more than that, but I am getting ahead of myself.

So, I spend my nights pottering, tinkering, tidying up around the place as best I can. I also spend a lot of my night-time making sure the guests are safe and well, looked after, cared for. They can become restless themselves and restlessness can become dangerous when they are in the state that some of them get into. Perhaps if I explain - no, I will show you an example, come with me now, but don't be too loud - it can scare some of them.

Let me start by saying we do not judge anyone here. We don't make comments that harm, we don't say negative things and above all else we do not judge. For after all who are we to judge another, another's choices, another's path in life. I've heard so much nonsense recently about 'journeys' and 'my story' – and it is all just that – nonsense. You don't start a life thinking 'that's the journey I will take', 'that will be my story' – as a child you have ambitions, hopes, dreams, and you try to follow them. It's unfortunate but most people do not achieve their hopes, their dreams – they just don't – that's a fact. So, what does that leave you with? Coping? Doing the best you can? Probably. But doing the best is not about making do, it's about being the best you can be where you are, and when you are. That's not coping – that's enjoying – living.

Look at me. I know you don't know me that well, but believe me, I have been around. I have seen things and done things and I have to say I am not proud of some of them – I don't think anyone would be. But I am where I am, and I have to say overall I am quite happy with the life I have.

I suppose, in my position I must be as happy as I can be. I've been around forever it seems, and I know, unless anything majorly untoward happens in the cosmos then I'll be around for an awful lot longer. Longer than any of my guests and probably longer than you, Weary Traveller. You see my guests are just passing through. I live here, I am here, but well they just pass through. They have the option to stay if they want, or they can carry on their 'journey', their 'story' if they so choose – as I say we do not judge here.

Anyway, here we are at number 20. Prepare yourself because it may not be a pretty sight, but just remember, 'judge not, lest ye be judged' as my mate Matthew once said. I open the door and the first thing that hits me is the smell. I try to keep my guests as clean and fresh as I can, but some of them, well, they have the propensity to 'go off a bit' I think is the politest term. Oh, they're not rotting away or anything – just perhaps not taking as good care of themselves as maybe they should. I'll get Lorna in here later this morning – ah, sorry I didn't tell you Lorna also doubles as a maid here. I know, you're thinking exploitation, but it's not I assure you; she does live rent free, and for free board and lodgings she must do something. Otherwise, she'd just sit around and mull over her 'journey', her 'story' and we couldn't have that - Lord alone knows where that would lead. I think Lorna may have her work cut out in number 20 as, when I approach the bed, the occupant stirs, and it would appear he has let things go a bit more than I first thought – we'll be brief – it can be a bit overpowering if you're not used to it. This is Tommy Zeitz…. yes, I know, I know, he's let himself go a bit, but, and please keep this to yourself – young Tommy here is not as youthful as he used to be and obviously after the horrific football injury he suffered, things have gone a bit downhill for him. You probably read about his latest run in with the law, his third wife divorcing him, again, and that scandal that fortunately for him was only on the paper's front pages until that shooting – you know the one, the one in that shopping mall – with the .... well never mind. This is Tommy Zeitz. Tommy first passed by the motel, oh, about a year ago, and well, he just sort of stayed, on and off. I don't mind, it's nice to know you're helping a celebrity get back on his feet, even if it might be taking a little longer than I thought it would. I offered him a week of rest and then laid out a plan for him, but the weeks rest turned into a month's rest and then I didn't see him until he returned with two young ladies who, shall we say, were not the sort you'd take home to an ageing mother - I'm sure you get my point. Anyway, I let him have a couple of days of fun and then got rid of them.

Tommy had come to see me at the diner one afternoon and we had sat and talked.

"Hey Eddie , how's it going?" he casually enquired.

"Time passes Tommy, time passes. More to the point, how are you? Your bed was not slept in last night".

"No. Sorry about that. I stayed up chatting with another inmate and, well, one thing led to another. But hey – her bed wasn't slept in much either – at least not till much later – know what I mean? Anything for breakfast – worked up an appetite – get my gist?"

"Oh, indeed I do Tommy. I will get you something for breakfast, although in some countries this particular meal would be called lunch, or even an afternoon tea. I won't be a moment". I rose and a few minutes later I returned with the largest greasiest breakfast someone like me can create in the time allotted and set it before him.

"Bon Appetit, young Tommy. Your story starts again today I think?"

"Yeh, yeh, sure - Jesus Eddie - is this all for me?" he asked.

"Oh yes" I assured him "where you are going, you will need a full breakfast inside you - it may be a while before you eat again".

"Yeah. About that Eddster…..look I've been thinking….maybe give it another couple of days - you know, let the dust settle?" Tommy said as he ploughed into his bacon and hash browns.

"Tommy. You have had more than a few days, there has been enough dust settling and, unless you tell me otherwise, you are not getting any younger. And you will need as many of your faculties which remain to assist you on your onward journey, don't you think?"

"Well, yeh, sure…I was just meaning…."

"And again, correct me if I am wrong, but your energy can be expended when you want it to be…"

"Oh yeah - no issues there !"

"And so, we just need to channel that energy, that drive if you will, to get you back on the right path?" I put to him.

"Yeh, sure. I understand. We had a deal" he said into his beans.

"We did indeed. And, when you've finished your repast we will begin. I'll put something appropriate on the jukebox shall I?" I said as I got up from the table.

"Let's see, let's see….ah yes" I mused and pressed 12B.

At my touch a wonderful song rang out across the diner and caused Tommy to raise his head so quickly his fried tomato escaped on to the floor

The Charlie Daniels Band - The Devil went down to Georgia - wonderful !

A short time later the reception door had opened, and a replete Tommy Zeitz entered, belching as he did - such a charmer - why on earth I am helping him I do not know - still I do not get to choose, they do, and I do not judge…lest I be judged, and I wouldn't want that.

"Ah Tommy. Right on time. Are you ready? Have you prepared yourself?"

"Prepared myself? How the f..., how would I prepare myself for this? It's not a Superbowl for Christ's sake !"

"Oh no Tommy, it's much more than that, and not that I judge, you didn't have to prepare yourself for too many Superbowl's did you? Remind me?" I wasn't trying to be mean, I just thought at that time, he might be persuaded on to another path, and save us all the trouble of Tommy Zeitz MkII.

I remember at that time, unfortunately, or fortunately the doorbell rang again, and as it swung open a young man, with what I recalled was a haunted look on his face, entered.

"Hi ! Can I? Sorry, it's a bit tight in here, I'll wait outside - let you finish" he stammered and convinced himself.

"No. That is fine young man. Tommy. Can I ask you to take a seat in my office? And please, don't touch anything. Firstly, I will know, and secondly, I will not be happy. I will only be a few moments - please show the young man back in. Thank you"

"Yeh. Sure Eddie. I'll be…yeh…your office, sure" Tommy muttered as he left the reception.

The young man had returned and approached the desk with his head bowed. He looked like he owed the world a living, and perhaps he did, who was I to say.

"Hello young man. How are you today, though by the look of you something troubles you I fear?"

"Hi, yes. It does. I want…I need, a place to stay…not that I'm in any trouble you understand, just somewhere, you know, out of the way, for a few days, and nights obviously" he raced as he spoke.

"Certainly. Just passing through then? Not looking at going back? Sort things out at all? Whatever it is that you're not in trouble with?" I passed a registration card to him as I said "Sorry. Rules"

"No. No. That's fine. Erm…what shall I?…Who do I …?" he asked.

"I can't complete it for you young man, but let's say that you have a problem with writing things, for example, and were to dictate what details you wanted to have written for you - how does that sound?" I offered.

"Yes. Thank you. That would be good….my name is…"

"Just a moment. I don't think that pen writes properly. Now you were saying what name would you like written here on your behalf…?" I asked him.

"Oh right. I see…well then how about Marcus Bryson?"

"Oh good. Lovely and bland….and an address Mr Bryson if you will?"

"Bland? Why bland, that's the name of…."

"I'm sorry Mr Bryson, I thought that was your name - you do see what I'm trying to do for you here young man don't you?"

"Yes. Sorry - a bit nervous - I've …well, I've been through a lot you see?"

"Haven't we all Mr Bryson, haven't we all….now an address somewhere up country perhaps? A distance away may be - Chicago? Ohio?"

"Really? Why there? Do I look like I come from Ohio?"

"No. But perhaps Mr Bryson does? Let's put something middle of the road down shall we - a farm address perhaps - lots of them in Ohio - there, how's that?"

"Yes. That's good, thank you - you've done this before haven't you?.....Mr?"

"Eddie. Call me Eddie. Now, any idea how long you'll be staying - oh, and do you have a vehicle, does it need, perhaps protecting from the sunlight - it does get very hot here, and also dusty what with the winds, that can ruin a car's paintwork - perhaps if we put it out the back, under a tarp for the moment? Would that help?"

"Yes. Thank you….you've?"

"Been here before? Many times, Mr Bryson, many times. Now let's get you settled. Room 12 - have you any luggage? Probably not. I'll get the maid to sort you some accessories, toiletries, and the like - please follow me".

Chapter Six

I'm going a bit off track here aren't I? I told you I did that sometimes.

I started by telling you about the not so young Tommy Zeitz but that then led on to the man who wanted to call himself something bland, but still could only come up with the name of a friend, perhaps, or someone he knew? This was obviously his first time here, whereas with Tommy it definitely was not his first rodeo.

Let's leave Tommy now - he is in a sleep of sorts and goodness only knows what he is dreaming about, what he is experiencing where he is. His body is here, in my motel, but his mind, some would say his soul, is definitely elsewhere.

I showed you Tommy to let you in gently to what we do here. We help people. We give them board and lodgings - well, we don't give it to them - we exchange it for cash, or credit cards, but mainly cash. In exchange for the board and lodgings our guests get a second chance, an opportunity to put things right, if they so choose. It is unfortunate but some like Tommy in room 20 have been here a few times and just keep repeating the same mistakes and never quite taking the opportunities they are presented with. But, as I say we will come back to Tommy - we may have to move things along for him - it would only be fair.

Let me tell you another story - in fact, I started to didn't I? - It relates to the young man who came into the reception just as I was going to give Tommy his second or was it third plan - you know the one I mean - the one who we'll call Marcus Bryson.

Marcus came to us just once - he stayed a few days - laying low as he had wanted, but a few mornings later he walked into the diner. Let me tell you about it, as I remember it.

I was cleaning the pots and pans - it's something I don't get to do a lot - oh I clean them when I've used them, but it's only a quick wash and wipe, whereas on this day I was giving them a good scrub - I could almost see my face in some of them.

So, there I was, at the sink with my back to the counter when a quiet voice said.

"Excuse me…..Eddie?"

I turned and saw Marcus leaning up against the counter, still looking a little pale, but certainly less haunted.

"Good morning Marcus. Nice to see you up and about. How are you feeling?" I asked him.

"Still awful…about what happened, but, strangely, a little better. I feel like I've slept the sleep of the dead I really do" he said as he yawned into his hand.

"It's often the way here Marcus - I think it's the open air - it has that effect on people -

can I get you something - breakfast, coffee perhaps?" I offered.

"That would be great, yes, thanks - just coffee and toast please - I can't eat too much in the mornings".

"Coffee and toast coming right up. Fancy some music? Choose yourself a tune while we wait" I suggested to him.

Marcus went over to my Rock Ola and leant over the screen. Knowing people's 'stories', I play a little game with myself and try to guess what song they will put on. I try to think what I would want to hear if I were them - sort of put myself in their shoes and choose a song to either cheer me up, or to wallow in. I must admit I don't often get it right. I didn't with Marcus.

He returned to the counter and sat with a slump on a bar stool just as the dulcet tones of Jon Bon Jovi started up - Wanted Dead or Alive. Oh dear, this might be a long road with young Marcus here - he was still in a dark place. I'd have to think of a good plan for him. I had him down for Lynyrd Skynyrd and Freebird.

Marcus had eaten his toast and having downed a coffee we took another one each over to a table. There wasn't anyone else in the diner and as I had the paperwork with me I thought we may as well make a start for Marcus. I thought he was ready.

As he sat opposite me I could not help but be sorry for him. I know that I shouldn't feel sorry for these people, for my guests, I am only a host, a keeper of sorts but, well, he was only young, perhaps nineteen or twenty and he really shouldn't be here. He may have done wrong in his brief time on this earth, but everyone deserves a fair crack at a life and things people do often take time to be seen for what they are, whereas bad things - well, people are so quick to judge, that's all I'm saying.

"Marcus. You've been here a few days

now, and you look better, rested. Do you think you are ready? Have you read the literature we left in your room?"

"I have, yes. This is some sort of retreat - some sort of well-being centre then?" he asked.

"Yes. I suppose so, but it's not about yoga and centering your chi here - you understand that don't you? You know what we do here - you did read the brochure, didn't you?" I wanted to confirm he knew what he was getting into if he signed on the dotted line.

"Well," he began "I was tired when I picked it up, so I sort of scan read it I suppose but I get the gist. I sign up for a period of time and you give me another chance, but I lose some time when I come back…..? Is that about right"?

"Yes. Broadly speaking. Have another look at the brochure and then read, and I mean read, the contract here. I'll go and sort a few more pots and pans. Give me a shout when you've read it, yes?" I got up and walked back to the counter.

I thought that when I turned around Marcus would not be there. He would either not believe what we did here or doubt its effectiveness. Every system has a drawback - there are no totally fool proof schemes in the world, so I could understand his caution. But our literature was as transparent as could be - I'd written it myself. I had been writing it for years, in all forms, on tablets, on parchment and on paper and strangely now back on tablets - oh yes, we were quite up with technology here. In fact, we were a little ahead of Apple and Google if I were being honest.

Marcus surprised me by being there when I turned round but asked me to return to the table. He had a worried look on his face and I could tell he was having doubts. This was a non-starter, I knew, but he was a good lad and I felt that a clean no sale was so much better than a dirty one. I would not force him to make a choice that was wrong for him.

"Marcus. I sense you have some questions" I started.

"Yes. Can I ask…and thank you for putting me up for the last few days - I know you are quite full at the moment" he said

I looked casually around the diner and coughed…"Erm, not really, but please, do go on".

"Can I ask? I've done what I've done, and I think I know the consequences of what will happen to me when I turn myself in - a lifetime in prison is the only outcome I can see …isn't it Eddie?" he almost pleaded.

"Marcus. No. Prison does not await you if you continue on your journey. There will be no three squares and an hour in the sun for you. No sewing of fishing nets and writing to your mum. No. Why do you think that?" I did feel sorry for him - he was not aware of his situation, not aware at all.

"Eddie, please help me - tell me what to do. I've never been in this position before, I've no idea what I should do - please advise me" he said.

"Marcus. I cannot advise you; I'm just not allowed to. All I can do is lay out the options you have. It is not for me to tell you what to do. You can carry on the path you are on and see where that takes you, though there are not a lot of options I have to say. Or, and I am not on a commission I assure you; you can sign up with us and we will take care of you. We have a number of plans for you to consider - the thing is only you can decide. I am not allowed to highlight the good points of what we do here, without alerting you to the risks and dangers you may face if you do proceed. I just can't. Think of me as a stockbroker, but with time as my currency. If you invest with a stockbroker you have to completely trust them, and they will do their best with your money. But they are at the behest of all sorts of outside influences and your investment could go down as well as up. With us, well, let's just say some people invest a lot of time with us, and have a great second chance, a wonderful experience, until their proper time comes - do you see? I would love to help you make the right choice, but I can't. My advice, for what it's worth would be - err on the side of caution. If you are not sure this is the right thing for you, then it probably isn't."

"But I got sent the brochure - why would I get sent the brochure if they didn't think it was right for me?"

"Marcus, everyone in your position gets sent the literature. Its standard practice - we target our market like every other industry - but it's not for everyone. Some people have very definite views on it and just throw our brochures away. Other people read them and then throw them away, and some, like yourself, actually come here. But, as I say, it's not for everyone and many are at peace with their chosen path, as you may be. As I say, it's entirely up to you".

"Eddie. You've been so good to me. You've taken me in when you didn't have to. You've not asked a lot of difficult questions, and just accepted me for who I am, for who I say I am, and never batted an eyelid, and for that I really thank you" Marcus said.

"That's fine Marcus. Just say 'thank you but no thank you' and we can settle up and you can be on your way, no hard feelings" I calmly said. I was disappointed as I knew this boy's future now - it's just that he didn't yet.

"Eddie. I'm really sorry. I just can't. I don't know, perhaps I should, but it just doesn't feel right - you hear so many scare stories - like timeshares, pyramid schemes and things, you know?"

"A totally different type of venture I assure you, but yes, I understand your hesitation, if that's your mindset. Look Marcus. There really are no hard feelings - you have to make the decision that is right for you, not me. I will carry on, and so will you - just on a different path. Come on, let's get you on your way then before you change your mind and make the wrong choice. I'll get your car and if you see Lorna at the reception, she'll sort your bill. OK?" I stood and shook his hand.

"Thank you Eddie. Sorry " Marcus said, as he also stood , and, wiping his face against his sleeve like a child with a runny nose walked away and was gone forever.

I read in the papers some weeks later of a young man's tragic story and knew it was the boy I had been speaking to. The one in the news had got his childhood sweetheart pregnant but her parents had not reacted well at all. They had banned their daughter from seeing the boy again and were looking at sending her away to distant relatives. The boy had taken it so badly that he had then shot and killed the parents. The tragedy was compounded some weeks later when the girl miscarried the child and then had taken her own life in desperation.

The boy then chose as his path of choice - 'death by cop' as the expression now is termed. In a standoff lasting some hours all efforts were apparently made to end things calmly, but the boy had previously decided the outcome and exited the building shooting wildly into the air. Unfortunately, the police were more targeted in their aim and the boy died in a hail of bullets.

I had kept Marcus' paperwork for a few days after he had left my diner. He honestly had thought he was still alive and could just give himself up to the authorities. The plan I had offered Marcus, or Mark Bryant as he was more likely called was a one month for six-month affair. Very reasonable I thought, but too much for him in the end and so he chose to continue on his own path.

Chapter Seven

It was sad what happened to Marcus, or Mark, as he probably was called, but as I've said I mustn't get too attached to my guests really, but it's hard sometimes. I've been doing what I do for a long time and sometimes it's hard to stay distanced.

It's when you see the Tommy Zeitz's of this world coming back over and over again - they're like cats with their nine lives they really are, and then you get people like poor Marcus choosing as he did, well it just doesn't seem right, it doesn't seem fair.

Excuse me a moment, there goes the door again.

"Good afternoon Sir. How can I help you today?" I enquired of the man before me.

"Is this the place?" he asked whilst looking around my extensive foyer.

"It's a place, certainly. What place was it you were looking for?" I said back to him.

The man looked windswept and a little fraught, as though he had been standing in a gale for too long, and perhaps living outside for a while. His clothes were ragged and dirty, and he had needed a wash and shave for about three weeks by the looks of things. Not my usual type of customer, but it takes all sorts - I do not judge. That sounds bad, I don't mean it like that, but that's how he looked - rough and very worn down around the edges.

This man had obviously come from somewhere recently that had been traumatic for him - I would get to know his 'story' soon enough - all it would take was just one touch.

"I've got this brochure, it says…..it says you can help me?....please?" The man placed a crumpled-up piece of paper on the counter and then slumped to the floor.

I went quickly through the hatch and lifted him to his feet. There was a small chair in the foyer, and I placed him in it. I stood back a shade as this man had an aroma all of his own, and when I had lifted him….his 'story' had come to me so suddenly, so clearly it was shocking - literally.

It was obvious to me that this man would need a lot of care and attention to help him back to the right path, well - a path that was right for him anyway.

"I didn't know……I thought it was right…..buy, buy, buy…I thought that's what I should do…oh God, oh God, what have I done, those poor people, I'm so sorry " the man was mumbling to himself, or possibly to me, it was hard to tell. At the moment this man needed a long bath, a shave and something to eat, and then a while to rest. He needed time to think and make the right choice.

I called Lorna at the diner and between us we half walked, half carried this poor soul to a room - 19, as he was likely to be here a while.

All of these rooms were fitted out in the same way. A double bed in the centre, a bedside cabinet either side of it, and lights above the headboard - the usual hotel / motel set up.

We differed slightly from other places in that there was no TV in the room and no electrical points. When people came here they needed to rest, before going on, or going back, as they chose. What they didn't need were outside influences or distractions affecting their recuperation or thought. No. No TV's, no radios, no mobile phones - they were taken from the guests when they checked in, terrible things - mobile phones - I would get rid of them all, if it were down to me.

We also differed from other establishments in that on either side of the bed was a metal clasp and ring, which we used to secure the guest to the bed, at least for the first couple of nights.

I know this sounds barbaric and all those other terrible things you're thinking right now, but I assure you - in my experience, and you will appreciate that that is a lot, this was absolutely necessary. We have always done it and it has saved lives I can tell you - trust me.

After the first couple of nights, we let the guest choose if they want the 'cuffs' or not, some don't, but some find them reassuring and continue to use them.

Lorna and I helped the man onto the bed and applied the cuffs. He was almost delirious anyway and so we made the choice for him. I would come and check him throughout the evening and night. I don't really sleep - I think I told you that.

The man had no car out front and so I presumed he had walked here. There weren't many cab firms that would come this far out, so unless he had hitched or caught a bus he must have walked. I think this man had been thinking of his own fate for some time bearing in mind how he looked, and to have walked here showed determination. Perhaps he was having second thoughts about his direction - we would let him rest up for a few days and see what he wanted to do.

While the new guest rested I went back to my office to do a little paperwork - oh yes, even in my trade there is paperwork. There was the motel side of things - the maintenance, purchasing, and stock taking from time to time, and keeping the IRS off my back was an ongoing battle, but it was the other role I played, the main reason I was here - that's what really took my time, office wise.

Let me fill you in a bit, sort of take you into my confidence a little, you seem the sort of person I could talk to.

You see the paperwork in a role like mine is immense. People talk about, 'I'm up to my neck in paperwork' well, I was literally drowning in it. For each person who went back, changed things, and came back, there were consequences, and these consequences had to be evened out over a period of time - sort of a smoothing of the ripple effect if you will. I have to record all the changes and see how I can move things along and smooth things out.

For example - you know that Deja vu feeling? - that's me that causes that. The feeling that you've been here before, but things are just a little off. - Me. You see, I am the ultimate timekeeper. I don't mean I have an enormous stopwatch and tut tut when people are late - no. I am a Timekeeper - that's my role, that's my job description and it is a full-time occupation I can tell you.

But there is nothing in the rules that says I can't have help - with the admin side of things at least. And in recent years, with people living such busy lives, and everything being online, and everyone linked to everyone else, I do get bogged down in paperwork.

You see, as you will have gathered I provide a service here - I say I, but it's a team effort really. I have Lorna to help me at the moment, she helps with the diner and cleaning as you know, and she is likely to be here for a while, and then there is my office manager Mike who also doubles as a handyman as and when needed. Let me tell you about Mike - or rather why Mike is still here after all this time.

It was a while ago, probably ten years since Mike first came here, he was in a sorry state as a lot of people who find themselves in my foyer are, but he had something about him - he seemed at peace with himself, but you could see it had taken a lot out of him to get there.

Let me tell you - show you what I mean.

I was in my usual position, on the reception desk, feet up, thinking about nothing in particular when the bell rang, and the door opened.

"Good morning Sir, how are you today?" I asked of the man.

"Yes. Hello. Fine, thank you. I understand you have cheap gas?" He asked me.

"Yes, we do. The cheapest in a hundred miles" I assured him.

"Are the burgers good as well?" The man smiled at me.

"I cook them myself…..and though I don't eat them, I've not had any complaints, well not so far". Some people intrigue me, and this man did. A lot of people who pass through here, or rest up a while, don't 'intrigue' me, their stories are sad, and in many ways predictable, which just makes them sadder. I do actually spend a lot of my time trying not to think, so when an intriguing customer comes my way, I try and, well I try and enjoy the experience. It keeps me occupied and makes the job worthwhile I suppose.

"OK if I stay a while?" The man asked outright.

"It's OK with me, just don't start a business from your room or have all night parties. Both tend to upset the guests, and the manager here is such a hard ass !" I joked.

"Great," the man smiled again. "Is there a form I need to fill in....and do you take cash?" He asked.

"Cash is the best currency Sir" I said as I passed him the registration card.

I sat back to give him some space to complete the form and also to avoid touching him, as I wanted to see how things played out with this customer. It had been a slow week and I had immersed myself in paperwork, so this man was an opportunity to get my head up, so to speak. If I touched him I would know his story, and where was the fun in that?

A few moments later the man passed the registration card back across the desk.

"Mike O'Halloran" I said, "Is that correct?"

"It is Mr???" Mr O'Halloran asked.

"Eddie - just call me Eddie" I said, "and you say that you are from Oregon?"

"I do say that Eddie, yes indeed" he replied.

"And do you know how long you'll be staying Mr O'Halloran?" I enquired.

"I don't at the moment. It depends. I feel I should just pass through just to spend some of the cheap gas your garage has and yet I think I might slow down a while, sort of take a few days - would that be OK Eddie?"

"Of course…Mike. Stay as long as you need. Is your car out front?" I asked him.

"No. I've taken the liberty of putting it around back, I hope that's OK as well?" he asked.

"Certainly" I replied, "would you like one of those burgers?"

"Yes. I would. Thank you" Mike replied.

And so, Mike came into the diner and seeing the jukebox asked if he could select a tune, which I said was fine, but to make sure it was upbeat. I was feeling in need of an upbeat song, but the song Mike chose made me stop my cooking, just to listen to the words. He chose Wrong Side of Heaven by Five Finger Death Punch - a stunning ballad from a most unlikely source. Only one person had ever played that song in all the time I had been here, and that person had been me.

"This one OK Eddie? Don't know if you know it?" Mike called from the Rock Ola
"Oh yes, Mike. It will do just fine. Burger will be just a minute" I called back.

I couldn't help but think, how did he know to play that particular song? Of all the choices he had, he chose that one song - what were the odds. I took him his burger and fries, with a side of slaw, obviously and a root beer as I thought he did not drink.
As I placed them on the table Mike looked up and said
"How did you know Eddie?"

"The same way as you knew to play that song Mike. You've been through this process before I take it?" I asked him.

"Once before yes. I had to set something right, but it cost me a lot. I don't want to go through that again and as I don't know how much time I have left I don't think I can afford to - do you? Did you want to shake my hand and then let me know what you think Eddie?" Mike said as he offered me his hand.

"No Mike. I don't want to interpret what I see. Tell me your story and then let's see what I can do for you - how does that sound?"

"OK. I will tell you my story".

Chapter Eight

Mike took a mouthful of his root beer, nodded to me, and began:-

"I was born in Ireland a while ago and brought up to respect my family. It was beaten into me, and I was never allowed to forget who I was or where I came from. My father was a violent man and used his fists on all of us, my brothers, my sisters and especially my mother. On a Friday and Saturday night he would come home from the pub and expect everything to be just so. And God help us all if it wasn't. To say that we were terrified of him would be the understatement of the century. We lived in squalor, but he expected it to be spotless - drunk as he was he would inspect every last corner of that hovel and woe betide us all if it wasn't clean. We would all get a beating for just a bit of dirt or soot on the floor - all of us. He would chase us round with his leather belt and not stop until all of us were wailing.

I had a large family, three brothers and three sisters, I was the oldest and well, my mammy just couldn't cope. She was a weak and frail woman when she was young but as she aged she got worse, so much worse. But my father did not care. He put on her so, even when she was sick or if she tried to refuse him, to push him away, he would beat her mercilessly.

I hated him but my mammy would not hear a bad word said against him and it wasn't until I was a bit older that I realised I had to do something about him before he killed her. He was never going to stop.

I worked every day and gave my mammy most of my wages - my father drank all of his and although she washed for half the street the money my mammy made also went down his throat. But he still expected her to provide food and clothing for us all just the same. It was impossible for her. I've no idea why she married him in the first place and I've no idea why she didn't leave him.

When I was about fifteen I was working as a runner for a bookmaker in the town. The pay wasn't great, but it helped my mammy and for that she was grateful. The bookmaker was not a straightforward man - he had all sorts of side-lines going on and as I was never stopped in the street he got to asking me to run all sorts of things for him.

This particular day the bookmaker asked me to take a gun to a friend of his. He'd wrapped it up in newspaper and stuffed it in a satchel, making it look like the usual betting slips run I normally did for him on a Saturday.

I took the gun and once I'd got around the corner I opened the satchel - I wanted to see what a gun looked like up close. Oh, I'd seen them before, the bookmaker and his men all carried them - it was a rough town I lived in, but I had never handled one before, never seen one this close up.

And so I took it out of the satchel and unwrapped the newspaper. I was in love - the weight of it, the smell of the oil on it and the feel of it in my hands - forget women, forget money - this, for me anyway at that time, was true love. From that moment, with that Colt in my hand I knew what I wanted to be, and I knew how to get it. I was young and naive and also I felt just a little bit invincible - well you would have as well - if you had seen that gun - blue black and so slick to the touch, so welcoming in the hand, it truly was exotic.

I knew the bookmaker was expecting me to deliver it to his man by a certain time and that if I did not arrive by then, then someone would come looking for me, but I knew what guns were for and I knew who this particular gun was meant for. You see, the man the bookmaker wanted me to take it to was a friend of my father's and I was to take it to a house just near ours.

113

By the time I got to the house though the lights were out, and I knew I had taken too long. I decided then to take the gun home and deliver it the following morning, I would explain that I had been delayed and I was sure the bookmaker would understand.

And so, on that fateful evening I arrived home but as I walked up the stairs to our place I heard a row like I had never heard before, plates and glasses were being smashed and it sounded like the whole family was involved. My brothers and sisters were only little - between five and twelve years old and so I ran up those stairs taking them three at a time. I knew what I must do.

As I burst through the kitchen door I saw my father holding my mammy from behind, by the hair. She was twisting and turning and trying to get away from him and digging her nails into his hands and trying to bite him to get him to let go. Whilst she was frail she was also a tiger when provoked, but I thought this was a fight too far for her and so I pulled the gun from the satchel and aimed it at my father.

I expected him to stop, I expected him to tell me to drop it or there would be trouble. What I did not expect was him to laugh in my face.

I must have looked ridiculous though, standing there in our kitchen waving this pistol about like some gangster shouting all sorts of things at my father, and all he did was laugh more - every insult, every swear word, he just laughed. He would not stop. All the while he laughed at me and all the while my mother was pinned in front of him, desperately trying to get away from him.

I was so angry I cocked the weapon and holding it in two hands assumed what I thought was the correct stance for someone about to fire it.

At this my father stopped laughing and looked directly at me. He told me to put the gun down, there would be an accident, someone would get hurt, but I was so angry with him, I knew what I had to do, I also knew that someone would get hurt - that was the point of all of this. There was no going back from this.

So, there I was, weapon cocked, my finger on the trigger and my father in my sights. I remember it was deadly silent as all three of us stood there. The children had stopped as well, stopped their weeping and wailing and were all just standing there, in that tiny, cramped foul smelling kitchen in that hole of a town, waiting. They were all waiting for me, to do something. I wanted my father to leave, and I shouted that at him, but he would not budge. He held my mother by the throat now and was using her as a shield. He was a coward I knew - he beat women and children, and I knew what I had to do - to save my mother, to save us, from this coward, from this animal. I knew I could take the shot - I'd seen it in films - my father was an enormous target and so I screamed at my mother to get out of the way. She was only small and I knew she would not be in danger. What I did not account for was how much of a coward my father actually was. I was losing my grip on the gun, my hands were sweating and shaking, and I knew I had to act quickly - I would only get this one chance.

As my mother pulled to one side I fired, but my father had taken hold of my mother and pushed her towards me. The bullet caught my mother full in the chest and she dropped to the floor. She was dead before she hit the lino.

My brothers and sisters started up their wailing as you would expect, but my father? Well, he just walked out of the house and away down the street. He did not say a word - just walked away.

I knew I also had to get away from this horrific scene. I ran to a neighbour and begged them to look after my brothers and sisters and whilst they had heard what had happened and saw the kitchen they made no comment - just gathered my siblings into their arms and took them away.

I knew then that I had options - I could run, or I could finish the job. And so, I went to the place I knew my father would be - the bar.

His wife had just been shot and killed by his son and that bastard sat in a bar with a whiskey in his hand talking to his mates like nothing had happened.

Like I had been doing it for years I walked into that bar, walked up to my father, and emptied the gun, another six bullets into the back of his head, as he sat there drinking his whiskey. And, like I had been doing it for years, I walked out of that bar and away into the night.

I headed for the bookmakers and told him what had happened. He was, shall we say, a little disappointed that I had not delivered the gun to his man, but understood that things took a turn, as things sometimes did, he said.

He took the gun from me and called one of his men. I was then taken by the ferry to the mainland and then on a ship to America and began this life.

There, that is my story Eddie".

I had listened to what Mike had told me. I knew that was not everything and so I said.

"But Mike, you have missed out a few things, haven't you? You've missed out the bit about putting it right, about the plan you signed up for?"

"I have Eddie, yes. But you know the rest, surely?" he said.

"I could shake your hand now, and I will know, but Mike - you went back didn't you? You returned to Ireland and put things right?"

"I did. I found a place like this across the country and signed a plan. I had no choice. I had left my brothers and sisters with no mother and no father. I could not provide for them and so the only thing I could do was sign a plan."

"But that is the worst plan Mike - what was the time off period?" I asked him.

"Twenty years" he looked at me "Twenty years".

"And when did this all happen Mike? When did you kill your parents and then bring your mother back? How long ago?"

"Nineteen years ago," he said, "I think I have one year left".

"I have to ask you Mike. You are not my regular type of customer, and it would appear you have not arrived here by the conventional route? How did you come by the other place and then this place?" I was intrigued.

"I always kept in touch with the bookmaker - you know, to send my brothers and sisters some money when I could, through him, and he sent me a brochure one time and told me what you, and those like you can do for people. This place? Pure chance - the cheap gas actually, but when I walked into the diner I knew. I knew, as the other place looked exactly like this one" he explained.

And that was ten years ago. Mike is still here, putting things right for other people. He is now my office manager and occasional handyman, and will be until his time comes, and who knows when that will be. I do not shake his hand; I do not ask him how he is. He has never returned to Ireland since putting things right and cannot. He has not seen his family since that terrible time and will not, ever again. That was part of the plan he signed. Twenty years and never go back - that was a rough thing to have to do, but the rules are the rules, and we all have to abide by them.

Chapter Nine

It was maybe appropriate, or what was the word? - Freudian, that I ended Mike's story talking about rules, and how we all had to abide by them, for the next day I received a letter that was to sorely test me, and my position.

I had been in the diner when the postman stopped outside, his yellow van bright against the dark sky. Perhaps its colour was a foreboding - a warning of darker days to come. Whatever it was, Frank, the postman came into the diner.

"Morning Eddie - how's time? " He asked , as he always did.

"Passing Frank, time is passing" I replied as I always did "coffee?" I offered him.

"won't say no Eddie, think a storm's brewing out there" he observed.

"Very probably. Best to stay here a while. Breakfast Frank?"

"Be rude not to Eddie, thanks" he said and made his way to the Rock Ola

"Frank. Be imaginative today please - no Carpenters - Please Mr Postman, no Elvis - Return to Sender. Be creative ?" I almost begged him. For years now Frank had come into my diner and put on Postal related songs, time after time - so much so that I had taken to unplugging the jukebox whenever I saw his van.

As Frank sat at the counter and awaited his eggs, over easy on rye toast, I think I wished for those cliched songs he had chosen - for out of my own Rock Ola poured the gravelly sound of the late great Johnny Cash singing Bad News. I didn't think I had many of his tunes, but here it was and like its singer, Frank often brought me bad news.

I paid all my bills online and I rarely got advertising mail, and so when Frank came with the post it was usually bad news as the Man in Black was telling me. I placed Frank's breakfast in front of him and in return he reached into his mail bag and handed me a thin brown envelope.

"Look at the post mark" he said as he started to eat.
"There isn't one" I pointed out "oh no"
"Yep. No post mark - you know what that means - Head Office calling you Eddie - what have you been up to?" Frank tilted his head.

I put the letter against the till "I'll look at it later Frank. Now. Coffee" I said as I leant on the counter as Johnny faded out.
I walked out from behind the servery - I had to get Bad News out of my mind. I randomly pressed buttons and out came a song I hadn't heard for years - a real celebration song - I'm Still Standing by Elton John. It got a sideways look from Frank, but I didn't care. I'd always loved this comeback song - about a guy who had

been kicked about by nearly everyone and had just returned fighting, stronger and more determined than before. Oh, I wished that was how I felt - if I ever met Elton I'd ask him how he did it, but for the time being I just returned to my counter and stared Frank down, back into his free breakfast - give me the side eyes - huh !

Frank left a short time later and having cooked a few breakfasts for some actual paying customers, I knew I had to deal with the letter.

It was a letter from Head Office, and that was never good news. It might not be terminal news, fatal news, but it would not be good news for sure. I opened it and read its contents, brief as they were:-

Dear Etu,

Please present yourself at Room 101 at 10.00 on Wednesday 5th February. Please bring your section's up to date figures so they may be discussed by The Panel upon your attendance,

Regards

The Panel

Oh God, this was worse than I thought it would be. If The Panel wanted to see me, I could be in trouble. Well, thinking of Elton once more, I vowed to myself that I would come out fighting, I would go on the front foot and take the battle to them. I wasn't going to go down without a fight. I went to the office and spoke to Mike.

"I need the figures for the last quarter Mike" I said.
 "The last quarter?…OK I have them here somewhere, did you want the last quarter's figures, like the actual ones….or? " He hesitated.

"I've got to go to Head Office, so the ones that will make it look like we're holding our own in difficult times. Those ones" I let him know.

"Right. Give me an hour Eddie?" Mike said.

"Lovely Mike, I knew I could rely on you. I'm obviously going to be out of town for a little while. Whilst Lorna is officially in charge, you will be, but remember, don't answer the phone and can you put a note in reception telling people to go to the diner? " I advised him.

"Yep. Got it Eddie. Will it all be OK do you think? Will we all be OK?"

" I hope so, Mike. I will do my best" I said as I turned around.

The letter said 10am on the 5th, so I had two days to prepare myself, two days to convince myself that things would be fine, we would be OK, but the way I felt right now? Would we?

I had a look at my business through a critical eye - what would people see as the issues? What would they think I was failing on? I thought I was doing a good job - sure, I had turned away some would-be customers, but for the right reasons. I couldn't accommodate everyone, this was not for everyone, and it wouldn't be right, it wouldn't be ethical to get everyone I saw to sign up for a plan. I wasn't that sort of salesman. I had no actual targets to hit, mine wasn't that sort of business but I knew that Head Office would look at things a different way. They did not see the people involved. They did not have to hear the stories, look into these people's eyes, and see their pain - no, they sat in their ivory towers and….no. Stop it. I wouldn't go down that route. I would look them in the eye and explain my business. I would tell them the reason why I was good at my job, why I was the best person to do it, and that there was no one else who could do it.

The next morning, I set off for Head Office. It wasn't near, it wasn't far, but I decided to drive anyway. It was a bright day and I thought I could do with the wind in my hair and the feel of the open road was one I had missed for a while.

I had a 1969 Pontiac GTO which I kept stored out the back of the motel, but I did not drive it enough. I didn't actually need to drive today but I wanted to, and as I pulled out of the car park and onto the highway I considered turning left, rather than right, and just keep on going. But it didn't matter which way I drove, or for how long. The Panel had called, and they knew where I was. I could drive left or right, or forwards or backwards, it didn't matter. It was best just to get this over with and take what was coming square on. And so, with that in mind I drove for a few hours up the highway, listening to the radio stations as they changed, as they grew louder and stronger, and then weaker and faded. I listened to country, to jazz, to blues and then rock. I didn't mind - I was where I enjoyed being the most - out and about, free as a bird.

I stopped, curiously enough at a diner just as it was getting dark, for no other reason that I wanted to compare notes. I wanted to judge myself against other businesses and see how I was doing. Oh, I know my business was not what others were, and that my diner offered a little more than burgers, chilli and on occasion, spaghetti, but I felt a sort of kinship with other establishments and pulled in to assess things from a customer's point of view.

The first thing I noticed was that the gas was more expensive - I looked at my speedometer and saw that I had put nearly two hundred miles on the clock, perhaps I did have the cheapest gas around.

I would fill up for the return journey but for now I thought I would sample the delights of this place for the evening and continue in the morning.

I got out of my car and locking it I looked over the roof at the run of rooms laid out in front of me. About twenty nondescript chalets - the optimum number for a roadside motel. There was a diner with neon lights flashing - a bit gaudy I thought and not necessary, in my opinion, but, hey, each to their own.

I went into the reception and spoke to the woman behind the counter.

"Hi" I began "I wondered if you had a room, just for the night please?"

"Sure," she said, "just passing through?"

"Yes...I'm going to …..Rock Falls - do you know it?" I said.

"Rock Falls, Colorado? I've never been myself, but I'm told it has lovely views this time of year. What takes you there? Work? Business? Sightseeing?" She seemed genuinely curious.

I could not resist and so I said.

"Oh. I'm throwing my wife of a cliff there tomorrow".

Without batting an eyelid, the woman looked at me straight and said.

"Yeh. A lot of people do. Just a single then?"
"Yes. Just a single please. Is it too late for something to eat, and perhaps a beer?"
"Sure. Just need you to fill out a card - you know - usual details, and then we'll go over to the diner?" she said as she passed me the card. Our hands briefly touched and as she pulled her hand away she said.

"Oh. I'm sorry. Did you feel that…."
"Probably the carpet" I suggested.
"Probably. Yes. The carpet - Mr Dwight?"
"Call me Reg" I smiled at her.

Chapter Ten

The next morning, I pulled out of the motel car park and heading back the way I had come I put the radio on and listened to rock, blues, jazz and eventually country before pulling up just short of my own motel. I think you get the idea - I could drive anywhere I wanted but could not actually go anywhere. I was in my own little domain and could not leave. I was responsible for an area and was not allowed to leave it - not physically anyway.

I decided to carry on driving and put on a tape - my own choices and my own memories. I drove for another couple of hundred miles having filled up at a gas station past my own - more expensive, but money meant nothing to me in all honesty.

I thought I would pull into the next motel I saw and stay there until I had to attend the meeting. You see I could have attended it from my office, but it felt more like a meeting if I went 'out of town' for a few days - I had my position, my reputation to think of and I wanted my staff to see me as a businessman, rather than 'Good Old Eddie'. Good Old Eddie who never went anywhere, never did anything, never had a bunch of friends over to play poker, never shot the breeze and watched the football with them and a few beers on a Sunday. I wanted so much to be more than that person. I wanted to have friends, I wanted to talk nonsense about how well the Hawks were going to do this season and whether they should get a new line-backer or whatever the expression was. You see I knew nothing about football, nothing about baseball, nothing about any sports really and it saddened me. All American men knew about these things, but, well, I wasn't like all American men. I came before most of them, before the Fighting Hawks were founded and never really got into football or baseball. I couldn't see the point, there were so many other things to interest me, and I knew who was going to win each game anyway so there was no excitement for me in watching it you see.

I checked into the next motel and set up in a room away from the others. I wasn't necessarily shy, but I needed peace and quiet to attend the meeting. I did not want The Panel to think that I was away from my motel and so I wanted to keep any outside noises and suchlike to a minimum.

At just before ten o'clock I took out the mirror from my rucksack and placed it on the desk in front of me. This was no ordinary shaving mirror for example, but a portal, if you will - a way to connect with whomever I wanted and whenever I wished. I calmed myself, cleared my mind and waited.

At precisely ten o'clock the mirror flashed, and a face appeared. It was a Panel member and he greeted me. Whilst no words were spoken between us I will tell you what was said so you understand what

135

happened and why I would do the things I would, after this meeting. I don't mean to sound mysterious or bloat my own importance, but it was the way the meeting went that decided things for me and I can look back on that as the catalyst for all the things that followed.

"Etu. Thank you for attending this meeting" the Panel Member said - let's call him Terry for ease shall we?

"Good morning Panel. Thank you for inviting me - how could I resist?" I smiled to myself.

"You couldn't Etu - you know that" Terry said.

"Yes. I know - I was….never mind. How can I help The Panel on this fine morning?" I asked.

"Do you have your figures, Etu?" Terry said flatly.

"Yes. Here. I will pass them to you" I did not need to get them out of the rucksack - if I was honest I didn't need to bring them at all. I knew what the figures were - I had memorised them the previous night and it was that memory that The Panel were viewing now - scary huh?

"Interesting Etu - you seem to be keeping your head above water….just" Terry said.

"In difficult times?" I added.

"In difficult times" Terry replied "But these are not difficult times for you - you have seen many 'difficult times' as you say. These are again difficult times for mankind alone, are they not?"

"Well, yes. I meant that - difficult times, for mankind…yes" I trailed off "Was there anything specific I can help The Panel with today?" I enquired again.

"How is Tommy Zeitz doing Etu?"

"He's OK really. Taking a little longer than I had initially hoped, but I think he will do fine this time round and then, I'm hoping he doesn't need to come back again".

"Give him every opportunity to resolve his issues please?" Terry asked me.

"Certainly. Is there any particular reason why you are interested in Tommy. He's only a failed footballer? He blew out his knee a while back and fell foul to drink and then coke" I thought I was right in my summary of our Tommy.

"If that's what he's told you - if that's what he's shown you Etu?"

"It is. There is obviously more to Tommy than meets the eye. Can I ask what that something is?"

"You can ask, but we will not answer. Just give him time - the time he needs".

"OK? You're the bosses, but can you at least tell me how long I should give him, and how many times will he come back to me?"

"Again. Just give him time. Now. To other matters. The boy Marcus - why was he allowed to just go on with his journey. Was there not a plan that suited him?" The Panel asked me.

"I think with Marcus it came down to faith. I don't think he believed what we could do for him" I said.

"That is unfortunate Etu. Did you not find a plan for him? Could you not have encouraged him to have faith - encouraged him to have made the right choice" The Panel enquired.

"No. If I'm honest. I did not. I did not talk him into a plan. I could have, I know, I could have been 'that' salesman, but no. I let him decide his own path - surely that is what life is about?" I couldn't say too much more, or I would get myself into trouble.

"Ah" is all The Panel said. Just that one word.

"I'm sorry?" I began "Are you telling me that everyone has to have a plan? Everyone must have a plan. Surely each man chooses his own path?"

"So, Etu. You do not believe in destiny then - you do not believe in fate?" The Panel asked me.

"Yes. Obviously. I have been around too long not to, but each man has a destiny, each man has a fate - otherwise….you're saying this is all planned?"

"Do you think it is all planned Etu? Do you think there is a predetermined way for you for example?"

"If there is, then you would know it. Tell me now - is there a fate for me? Where do I end up?" I didn't like the way this was going.

"You will 'end up' as you so eloquently put it where you are meant to 'end up'. You're not like all other men, you know this. You help others choose their path, help them on their journey" Terry said.

I was getting a bit fed up with this to be honest. I felt The Panel were not happy with me - for some reason - because of Tommy. Because of Marcus? I'd been doing what I do for a long time, and I felt I was pretty good at it, and a pretty good judge of character - but I wouldn't talk someone into something I didn't think was right for them - was that the problem - figures? Really?

"Now Etu. The latest customer you've just checked in - we see there is no card attached to him - what do we know about him?" Terry asked.

"Not much to be honest. He collapsed in my foyer, and I've only just got him into a room. When we've finished here I'll look in on him and perhaps I can report back to you if there's anything about him?"

"If you would please - that would be… appreciated?" Terry let me know.

"Is there anything else Panel? Anything else I can do for you?"

"No. I think we're done. Thank you for attending Etu. Is there anything else you want to tell us? Anything at all? Anything you might have forgotten?" Terry seemed sure there was, but I wasn't going to make this easy for him.

"No. Not that I can think of - like what? I'm sorry? Have I done something to upset you? Something to cause you concern?" I asked them.

"No. Not at all Etu. I am sure that if you think of anything you will come back to us, yes? Keep us in the loop as they say?" Terry knew something.

"Well, yes, of course. So, if that's everything…..?" the mirror went dark - that was their reply.

This was the thing about some business meetings. You attend them with every intention of being honest - a 'I've got nothing to hide', 'they've got nothing on me' - type approach but about halfway through you think - maybe they do have something on you, or maybe they're just fishing, keeping you on edge, letting you know who is in charge - such a waste of everyone's time. If they were unhappy with me, perhaps they should just say - get it over with.

I thought they knew about Mike, I thought they knew about Lorna, and both would cause me problems. All I needed was a mystery shopper and I was done for. I would have to think about what to do. Maybe it was time to speak to Mike and Lorna about moving on - see what they thought.

I drove back to my motel and pulled into the rear car park. I put a tarp over my pride and joy and walked back into the office.

"Hey Mike. Anything going on?" I asked him.

"Hey Eddie. No. All quiet. No new guests. A couple of strange phone calls - hang ups - wrong numbers maybe, but no news. Guy in 19's awake - perhaps you could look in on him?" Mike said.

"Sure. Will do. Is Lorna about?"

"In the diner I think - with that Sarah lady. I've left them to it - girl talk's not my thing" Mike smiled. "Oh, and Eddie? That Sarah was in the office while you were away. Not doing anything - just sitting looking in her compact - sort of make upping I suppose?" "Ok. Thanks Mike" I replied. This was bad.

I left Mike and headed over to the rooms.

Chapter Eleven

I knocked on the door to number 19 - it's only polite after all - these were paying customers and they deserved a proper and courteous service during their stay here, however brief.

"Hello? Come on in, I can't get to the door at the moment, I'm a …bit tied up" a quiet voice came from within.

I opened the door and stepped inside. The room was dark and so I opened the curtains slightly.

"You don't mind?" I asked the guest.
"Larry" he said "My name is Larry, and please, yes open them… Could you also?" he rattled the cuffs.
"Certainly" I said "Just a moment. I hope you understand….why we…"

"Of course. I know I am a risk" Larry replied.

"A risk? A risk of what" I asked as I unlocked a cuff.

Larry sat up slightly and rubbed his still cuffed hand with his free one.

"May I have some water please?" he asked me.

"Yes. Of course," I unlocked the other cuff and Larry sat up fully on the bed. I got some water from the bathroom and returned to him.

"Thank you" he started "you're not what I expected".

"Expected?" I queried "what did you expect?"

"Well. I thought you would be…meaner, tougher…and I see you don't have a gun. You seem very assured" Larry said.

"A gun? Why would I need a gun? I think we need to talk - you can leave any time you like. Do you think I'm holding you here against your will? This is just a motel Larry" I explained.

"Sure. Sure. I've seen these types of places in movies - the motel in the middle of nowhere - the mild-mannered motel manager, talking nicely to the guy and then…."

"And then?"

"Blam !"

"Blam?"

"Yeah. You know…blam! Through the back of the head, or between the eyes. And you sort of have sympathy with the shooter, cos the guy probably deserved it?"

"Larry. Drink your water. Take a moment and then perhaps we will talk. Can I offer you some breakfast? Coffee. Orange juice?"

"Look mister. I know why I'm here and I do deserve to die - I've done a terrible thing - people have died because of me and I know the others have paid you to….to off me".

"Off you? No. I assure you, Larry, this is a respectable establishment - no one gets 'offed' here. They never have been and, whilst the motel is under my management, no one will. Would you perhaps like to take a shower, have a shave, and then meet me in the diner - I double as the cook as well as a hired hit man"

I got up and, leaving the door slightly open to show him I was not serious I left Larry to make his own decision.

About half an hour later Larry came into the diner dressed in the clothes I had laid out for him the previous evening. He looked a little more like a human being and as he sat at the counter he seemed calmer.

"This really is a diner then?" he asked.
"Yes. This really is a diner. And some would say I really am a cook, though not many. But, to continue our conversation no

one has ever called me a hit man before. Coffee?"

"Yes. Please, if I may - and you mentioned breakfast?"

"Certainly" I said and passed him a menu.

Larry chose the Dakota special - and as I prepared it I nodded at the jukebox - "help yourself - see if there's anything that grabs you".

Larry walked over to the Rock Ola. Now. He was a stockbroker - or used to be, something appropriate would be...money related - ah? Pink Floyd - Money? - no - too obvious. Steve Miller Band - Take the Money and Run? What was that Dire Straits one...about MTV or something? It would come to me. I was therefore surprised when the stockbroker put on The Bee Gees - Jive Talking - a brilliant song about lying but the singer having come to terms with it - people were strange.

"Larry - food's up" I called across to him over the upbeat song and he came and sat at a table. "Mind if I join you?" I asked.

"No. Not at all. Do I need to have a taster?" he smiled

"God. I would if I were you….no, I'm joking - it's fine - honestly, enjoy".

As I sat opposite Larry and stirred my own coffee I wondered what his story was. He had come here a couple of days ago, and according to Lorna had slept solidly since his arrival. He had had one of our brochures, and so that meant something, meant he had been offered our services and so I knew I had to speak to him, have 'that talk', but I was mindful of my meeting with The Panel. I wasn't going to be pressured into telling people what was best for them - they needed to decide for themselves, and I would only sell them a plan if it was right for them. I knew of others, like me, who worked in other areas - and were not so scrupulous? Was that a word - surely if unscrupulous was a word you could be scrupulous? Yes. I was scrupulous.

Larry was probably in his mid to late thirties but the way he sat, the slump of his shoulders told of a world of worries hanging over him and he seemed so much older. Guests who came here had all been through ordeals - otherwise they wouldn't be here - it was sort of an emergency room - a triage centre for those in desperate need.

We didn't mend broken limbs or pump stomachs here, but we still attended to the sick. We gave them a roof over their head whilst they decided what to do, where to go, and me? I was the A&E chief I suppose. It was down to me to decide what services we could give someone and then stand back, and let nature take its course.

"So, Larry. Hope your breakfast's OK? When you're ready, we can talk?" I said to him "I am Eddie by the way - I sort of run things round here".

" Hello Eddie" Larry said and offered his hand to me over the table.

"Oh, no. I won't, if you don't mind? Got grease all over me - one of the hazards of being a cook" I said and made a fuss of wiping my hands on my apron.

"So, are you ready to talk?" I asked, "I see you had one of our leaflets with you when you arrived?"

"Yeah. Weird that is. Like a cult thing , but in print? Wild"

"Yes. Wild. So, tell me Larry. What made you think I was going to…"

"Off me?"

"Off you. Yes"

"Oh, I don't know Eddie. It might have been being shackled to the bed for two days and all of that I suppose?" Larry said.

"I know it seems harsh, but it was for your own good. Did you read the leaflet? Did you see what we do here? You've been offered an opportunity, but you will need to trust, to trust someone, and that might as well be me? Or you can leave? I won't keep you here if you don't want to be here".

"Eddie. I didn't really get the chance to read the leaflet, but I think I understand. The last thing I remember is falling - falling from somewhere but then nothing, just being here, with that leaflet in my hand. I don't know how I got here - walked, I suppose, but from where? And where are we?"

"Somewhere in Dakota Larry. North or South - I forget? But you are safe, you are in good hands, and I will help you make the right decision for you. Tell me your story and then we can see what we can do for you?" I briefly touched his arm. I didn't get the full jolt I normally would if I shook hands with someone, but it seemed to wake Larry up a little.

"I was in finance Eddie. I was good, or at least I thought I was. I looked after people - made investments for them and looked after their money as if it was my own. Things went well for years. I'd come straight out of college and worked my way up in OCB - it was going well…"

"OCB?" I interjected.

"Ogilvy, Conner, Beecham?" Larry looked at me like I was from another planet.

"Oh yes. OCB - yeah I know……who?"

"One of the biggest investment houses in the country. I was at their New York office - I'd made it. I'd started off in various little, out of the way branches, but I knew, I knew, if I landed a few decent clients then Head Office would notice me, and I would move up in OCB".

"It's not always good to be noticed by Head Office - I can tell you Larry" I said.

"Anyway. The decent clients came in and they invested with us, with me. Do you know anything about finance Eddie - do you know about investments ?" Larry asked me.

"Not a clue - treat me like I know nothing - or, if you'd prefer, skip the financial details and give me a summary?" I offered.

154

"Sure. When a client invests with you, you are responsible for their money, and for them really - their happiness if you like - you sort of build up a trust and you have to have that - it's real important in my world"

"Mine too" I added.

"So, I had these clients - the Mannerheim's, and they invested heavily with me, but I don't know what happened, I don't know why things went wrong, but suddenly the markets started dropping - oh you can cover it for a while, move things around, use other people's money when clients start asking for some of it back. Some of them are actually quite knowledgeable about money, but they don't know everything and so they don't notice it. So, there I was moving client's money around to try and recover some of my losses, their losses, and I just sort of panicked. I thought I'd got it covered and eventually after a few months nearly everything was back to normal. I'd had a few lucky touches on Far East markets and so I managed to pay them back, the Mannerheim's, but they changed in how they were to me. I could sense that they suspected something. But they were greedy though and provided I kept making them money they kept investing, and so I got more and more ambitious, took greater risks, after all it wasn't my money and these people had loads of it. It didn't matter, I knew if it went wrong again I could just cover it again. A couple of months later I was happy once more, investing for new clients and I forgot about them - the Mannerheim's. They were still into me, and I kept investing for them.

I think I got lazy though, I started using clients' money. I've no idea what got into me, but I started working harder, longer hours to keep up, and I started with the coke - yeah - I know, same old story, but you asked, and I'm telling.

I wasn't sleeping and I was using it to keep me awake. There was more competition in the industry, and it was getting harder to keep ahead, and if you didn't keep ahead, you didn't keep clients happy, and if you didn't keep clients happy then you'd go under. I know, it all sounds like excuses, but this is what happened.

I'd got my move to Head Office, even got my own space, but I was called in to see Mr Ogilvy. I'd never met him before and so couldn't think why he'd want to see me? I'd been doing just OK for a newbie so I knew it wouldn't be good.

When I walked in there were all three of them though - Ogilvy, Conner, and Beecham. But with them was the firm's lawyer. He told me I had been named in a lawsuit and that OCB was dispensing with my services with immediate effect. Just like that - I was out. It turned out that the Mannerheim's had committed suicide. One had shot the other and then themselves, and all because of me. I had told them to keep buying and so they did. But they had made some enquiries and had found out what I was doing - they knew their money was so tied up with OCB, and that only I could untangle it for them. They had so much money, nearly all their money with us, and if they started taking it out to secure it, they wouldn't be able to do it quick enough to protect it. And so, they shot themselves. Because of me".

Larry stopped and looked up. He looked haunted by what he had told me.

"So, what would you like to do about it Larry?" I asked him.

"What would I like to do about it? I'd like to go back and stop them shooting themselves, is what I'd like. I'd like not to have their deaths on my conscience, that's what I'd like, but how can you ask me that? What else would I like? What sort of question is that?" Larry said.

"OK. Now. What if there was a way I could help you do that? Help you move on without the Mannerheim's on your conscience? How would that be?"

Larry looked confused.

"What? How could you possibly help me with that? Put things back as they were? You would have to turn back time to do that. You're mad" Larry exclaimed.

"I'll get you another coffee. Have a read of the brochure and when I come back we'll have a chat and see what you think" I told Larry.

A few minutes later I sat down again and saw that Larry had not only ingested his breakfast but had also taken in the information contained within our transparent leaflet. There were no holds barred, there was no glamour masking the small print - there was no small print - if only all businesses ran this way I thought.

"So, Larry. What do you think? Is that something you could go for?" I asked him.

Larry looked up at me, his mouth open, and then down again at the leaflet.

Chapter Twelve

I sat in the diner the next morning wondering what to do. I had a business to run, and people to look after. There were people here who I cared about - I know that sounds soppy - I am after all very old, and unfortunately I have seen many generations come and go, but you do become attached to people over time.

Lorna and Mike had been with me a while and I would hate for anything to happen to them. I thought I knew their histories and I also knew that neither really should be here, but I liked them around and so I had, well....let's just say I had bent the rules a little to make things easier for me as well as them.

Mike as you know had come through the front door like a lot of other customers and just well, stayed. He really shouldn't have if I'm honest, but as I've said to you he had something about him and so I made a few concessions in his timeline.

I'd made some enquiries about Mike O'Halloran and surprise, surprise I found nothing - absolutely nothing. I'd known for a decade that that was not his real name, but I'd never outright challenged him, I'd never made things difficult for him over the last ten years, but there had been consequences - things that happened that had had to be resolved over the years.

Mike and I had often talked into the small hours over a root beer or two and whilst listening to some great music. I often thought that my Rock Ola was haunted 'cos I'm sure that half the tunes we played were not on that machine, but by the mornings I didn't care.

One night a few years ago Mike surprised me and said he wanted to 'talk, talk'. I took this to mean it was something serious and so, root beers in hand and Rock Ola on low we sat at a table.

"Eddie, I need to make you aware of a few things about me, the real me" he began.
"Ah. OK Mike. One of those chats" even more intrigued.

Mike had kept himself to himself over the preceding years and I didn't know that much about him to be fair. I'd been fending off requests for any unauthorised people in my area - you know those who have actually cheated death, but try as I might, I couldn't find Mike in any of the reports that came from The Panel.

"Yeh. Eddie. You see, I am not actually Mike O'Halloran, but you knew that?" he asked.
"I did Mike. What do I call you then"?
"Oh, you can still call me Mike, but it's Mike Flanagan. And I'm not from Oregon either" he continued.
"I never thought you were. I knew you're from Ireland originally - at least that's what you told me when you came here, and your

story rang reasonably true - is anything else about it true though - the parentacide? Is that true? Did that happen?" I queried.

"Yes. That's all true. I did accidentally kill my mother, but I killed my father on purpose. But that's where the problem lies you see - the killing of my father".

"Go on. He is still dead; I take it Mike. He wasn't saved by a plan - no mysterious stranger suddenly dragged him to a diner in the middle of Ireland did they?" I said, still intrigued.

"No. He was well and truly dead when I left him. He won't be coming back, no. You see when I went to the bookmaker he said that as I had killed one of his men, I would have to take their place. I would have to take on my father's role that he had 'recently vacated', is how he put it - do you understand?" Mike looked at me and seemed troubled.

"I do see Mike. But what was so special about your father? What did he do for the bookmaker?" I asked.

"He was a hit man" Mike said quietly.

I couldn't help but laugh out loud - maybe it was the tension that had been building up, or maybe it was my remembering being mistaken for a hit man myself , whilst all the time I had one working for me - not Freudian….what would that be? I couldn't think - maybe just ironic?

"It's not funny Eddie. I am in trouble, and I don't think you can help me anymore. I know you've been pulling strings to help me stay on, and I really do thank you, but there are people who will come for me….they will kill me" Mike looked genuinely worried.

"No, they will not," I assured him.

"Yes they will. They are professionals - sent by the bookmaker to punish me for not carrying on with what he wanted. Since I've been in America I've been doing things for him, but I came to you as I'd had enough. I can't kill people anymore, I just

165

can't. I want a simple quiet life, nothing more, that's not too much to ask   is it?"

"Mike. The men came two nights ago, when you were in town - do you remember being in town?"

"Yes. You sent me to get some supplies - some…..I can't remember what it was….I can't   remember   getting them….you…you?"

"The men came, and the men left. That's all you need to know Mike. They will not be coming back, I assure you. You have your quiet life".

"What were the supplies I got - there's like, missing time for me that night…I don't remember. Why can't I remember Eddie - what did you do?"

"I made things better for everyone, well, for everyone but the two men who came here, obviously. But for you, you just forgot, and that's OK. You don't need to remember that night. Just forget it Mike and move on."

"What did you do? If you killed them there will be others Eddie - did you kill them?"

"No. I did not kill them. They shot each other. They had a burger, they had a root beer, and then they shot each other in the car park."

"Why would they do that Eddie? Why would they shoot each other? It doesn't make sense".

"I really don't know Mike. Who can say, but all I know is they came looking for you and left empty handed, maybe one blamed the other, maybe they fell out - who knows the mind of the hired killer…well obviously you do, but you get my point - I have no idea why people do what they do. Let's just have another root beer and talk about something else? What do you say?"

"I say Eddie. I say that two hired guns don't just not come back from a hit and 'we all move on'. The bookmaker will not let this go…what happened to the bodies? What did you do with the bodies?"

"Lorna and I disposed of them".

"What? A waitress in a diner 'disposed of them'? What the f…?"

"She's a cleaner as well Mike don't forget, and well, she cleaned the car park - I asked her to help me clean the forecourt and she did - I can be very persuasive when I want to be"

"Jesus Eddie ! Didn't she argue? Didn't she ask why?"

"No Mike. She did not. The same way that you cannot remember getting supplies for me, Lorna cannot remember putting two bodies into my truck and driving them out to Rock Falls".

"Rock Falls Colorado?"

"Yes. Lovely views, now I've seen them, they really are. I can see why everyone goes on about it. Wonderful scenery"

"Christ Eddie! And what? You just what? Threw them over a cliff?"

"Well no. Pushed, Mike. Human bodies are so very heavy - it's probably why they call it a 'dead weight'. Lorna and I sort of pushed them over the edge. It was dark when we got there, but the sunrise Mike, oh you should have seen the sunrise".

"Eddie. I cannot believe we're sitting here talking about…."

"Killing people Mike? Go on then, tell me you're not happy. You've killed people before - and what do you do with them when you've killed them. We said a few words for them - did you ever do that?"

"Well no. There's often no time. I don't really know them…."

"Well then. And I don't want to sound pious here but at least I said a few words for them, and don't forget I didn't actually kill anyone - they shot each other, remember?"

"But again, why?

"And again. I personally don't know the mind of a hired killer - maybe they were persuaded, who can say? Another root beer Mike?"

That hadn't been the only time people had come looking for Mike. I suspected that The Panel were on to him, and therefore

169

me, and were directing people to remember that Mike Flanagan still lived and that with a price on his head worth collecting they should really get around to wiping him? Or slotting him? Offing him - that's it, sorry, offing him. And I really couldn't allow that - he was after all a really good handyman and so happy in his work.

I still think that Rock Falls is a great place to see the sunrise - do go if you get a chance, but perhaps if you looked around at the bottom of Rock Falls you may feel it's getting a little over populated - certainly I've added about a dozen people to the area, but, and I say this in all honesty - I've not offed any of them.

Chapter Thirteen

Lorna was a bit more complicated - or rather her story was. Here we go again, his story, her story. And journeys? Everyone's on a journey aren't they? To where though I ask myself, and will they know when they get there? As they pull into their own particular station will they know, and will they alight the train and say 'phew, made it - what a journey!'

Anyway, sorry, as I was saying - Lorna herself was a young, fresh, easily influenced girl of twenty-three. And as I've already told you she fell for an older man and got into a bit of trouble - perhaps if I explain, and then you will know why I have a particular soft spot for her. I shouldn't really, it can be very dangerous in this industry to make decisions based on feelings, on emotions, rather than cold hard facts.

Lorna lived with her mother Elise, and grandmother Estelle in a little house in a quiet street and had a simple life. She loved her mother and grandmother and looked after them as best she could, running errands for them and putting by as much of her wages as she could, to help out and to ensure that all their ends met at the end of the week.

Estelle was elderly in your years, though not by mine - no, in mine she was a young thing, only about ninety, but she still got about. She still went to the local dances, although she no longer got up and threw herself about like she used to. Nowadays she sat and tapped her feet and bobbed her head to the music. In her younger years she had been such a dancer, I remember dancing with her so many times in the village hall - such nights. I do miss those evenings when Estelle and I danced into the small hours. I used to walk her home hand in hand, hoping for a kiss when we got to her door. But it never came. The nights never ended as I wished they would. No. With Estelle all I got was a handshake and a wave as she went up the steps and into her house.

Over the years I moved about a lot and gradually lost touch with Estelle. I read about her getting married and having a daughter and whenever I checked in on her she seemed happy. I used to change my appearance and she never recognised me, but I still saw the dancer in her, I still saw the sparkle in her eye. The husband left shortly after the child was born, but Estelle put everything she had into ensuring her daughter was happy. She wanted for nothing and maybe that was Estelle's downfall.

Her daughter Elise grew up to be a totally different woman - she was cold and harsh with people and whilst I wouldn't say she was uncaring, I never saw her dance, I never saw her throw everything into a jitterbug as Estelle had once done. She was distant with people and so they were distant with her.

I think Elise wanted to achieve great things but saw at an early age that she most likely wouldn't get anywhere near them and so in her frustration she became colder and colder with those around her, including her mother, which saddened me, as Estelle had given her only love.

Elise started to rebel, as children often do. She started staying out later and later and then not coming home at all. Whenever I checked in I saw how this affected Estelle, but I knew I must not interfere. It was not my role to change people's lives before they needed to be changed. I could not step in, halfway through a life - no, my job was for later on in their timelines. I felt inept as the woman I .....would it be loved? Alright. The woman I loved, was suffering and I could do nothing about it. I could not speak to The Panel as I knew they would just reassign these people to someone else and they would be lost to me for ever. I had no one to talk to about it and so year after year I could only watch as Estelle suffered and Elise 'pushed those boundaries' as the popular saying goes.

Surprisingly enough Elise got pregnant - some fumbling and grappling in a car apparently, and nine months later young Lorna was born. As before with her mother, the man responsible ran from his duty and left Elise with a child she did not want and a life to match.

Elise allowed me to step into her life on three occasions - the first was when she thought she should jump off a bridge to 'end it all'. She hadn't meant it I'm sure but had stumbled on the slippery ledge. She had signed up very quickly for the plan I put in front of her. No questions, apart from the obvious one and she was returned to the bridge and had walked away wondering why she was there in the first place.

The second occasion was when she tried to take her own life with drugs.

Another desperate cry for help no doubt, a situation that, until it actually happened I could not get involved in. Again, when the paperwork was put in front of her Elise signed it without reading it.

In total she had signed away twenty years of her life, just to keep going as she was - so sad really - she never changed her path - her 'journey'. She had been given two chances, more than the usual and I had put my neck on the line for her, especially with the second plan - there was some creative accounting happening in my office that day I can tell you, but I was doing it all for Estelle. I could not let her daughter die - it would kill her and although she didn't have many years left herself, what she did have should be as happy as possible. A suicidal daughter was not what she needed at this point in time - and so I bent the rules.

If you asked me now, I would freely admit I knew what I was doing was wrong, I knew I would get in serious trouble if I

176

was discovered to be interfering, but I could not let Estelle suffer.

As Lorna grew up I saw a lot of Estelle in her. She was not my child or concern, but I felt so close to her. I haven't been honest with you about Lorna though. I said earlier that she was a distant cousin - she wasn't, obviously. She was just someone I loved like I loved her grandmother and wanted to look out for.

Unfortunately for Lorna, whilst she had many of her grandmother's attributes she also had some of her mother's and she fell for the charms of an older man as you know.

I don't know much about love, but I realised quickly whilst keeping an eye out for Lorna that the man she had fallen for would only bring her trouble. The older man was her sister's husband, but she would not let it drop. He apparently kept telling her that he would leave his wife - her sister, but as the weeks and then months passed he did not, and she became more desperate.

Lorna begged him to leave her sister, threatened to tell her of their affair in an effort to make him leave her and he said he would. One fateful night some years ago he said he would tell his wife and that they would be together, that they would run away, and young, naive, desperate Lorna believed him. The man was rotten through and through and had been using her all along - he had no intention of leaving his wife - why would he? What prospects did he and Lorna have? Absolutely none.

Lorna had been parked in her car, a little way up the road from her sister's house - awaiting her lover to exit through the front door - his head held high and hopefully his arms full of his belongings - a sure sign that the deed was done. What Lorna actually saw was the man leaping out of a window and her sister launching items at him. What she heard was the man begging his wife to take him back, to forgive his 'silly fling' his 'moment of madness' as he put it.

Something inside Lorna snapped at that point - she knew then that he would never be the one for her, and that he'd been using her as a distraction from his wife.

The man approached the car he knew was waiting for him, with a smile and a wave for Lorna. But as he buttoned up his shirt and zipped up his fly a ton and a half of raging metal bore down on him and dragged him for a hundred yards before giving him up to the tarmac. Lorna screeched out of the road and onto the highway, blindly accelerating towards the bridge that her mother had once stood on and slipped off some years before. The irony was not lost on me as I stopped time and took out my paperwork.

I took Lorna and sat with her, Elise and my Estelle in their home and explained what I had in mind. It was clear that Estelle did not recognise me, but something in the way she spoke, said that she knew what I was.

She did not have many years left but freely gave them to extend the life of her granddaughter - she signed a plan there and then - she needed no persuading. Lorna had died on the bridge that her mother nearly fell from, and Estelle gave Lorna her remaining years. I think she would have given anything to the girl, but her ten years was not enough for this sweet young girl - she needed more.

Elise was a shadow of anything she used to be but was still a hard sell. She had shown me twice that she didn't want to live any longer but kept asking what was in it for her - what did she get in return?

With Estelle's help I had to persuade Elise that she could help her daughter have years of life, she could live a life away from here, away from the heartaches and troubles that she herself had gone through. I had nothing to offer Elise, and I would not lie to her. All I could do was play on her love for her daughter - it was a very hard sell.

Eventually Elise agreed that I look after Lorna, and take her away from the area, away from this life and offer her another. In return I gave her what she craved the most - oblivion.

And so, Lorna came with me, to my diner. She will not leave, she cannot, for if she does she will die. She will forever be twenty-three and though she doesn't know it she is the best she will ever be.

Chapter Fourteen

So there, I've told you about my staff, unofficial though they are - Mike and Lorna. I have a few others come in from time to time to keep The Panel happy, but Mike and Lorna are the main ones I look after and keep around to look   after me.

Mike - a hit man hiding from those wanting to kill him, for not killing others, and Lorna, who's only 'crime' was to love the wrong man, oh, and then run him down in her car.

You might think that I surround myself with killers, but I do not. Well as it turns out I have, but not intentionally. I am supposed to work alone and have for the main part been left to my own devices. I am responsible for a large area of America and do what I can to help people, as I keep telling you. The Panel knows that I set up a diner and use my skills to help those as and when they need help.

When the right sort of person dies, I am notified, and they receive a leaflet. They then have the option of coming here and seeing what I can offer them.

Some do and some don't. Those that don't, go on, and die the way they were about to - shootings, fires, robberies, traffic accidents and so on. They say that at the point of death your life flashes before you, and it's true - it's because of people like me and The Panel. We show you what you've done and then a little bit of what you will do if you choose to continue on your journey. In other words, you don't have to die - it will cost you, but you don't have to die.

You've probably read in the papers and seen on TV that someone had a 'miraculous escape' - they somehow 'survived the impossible' - again, that's down to people like me and The Panel. Those people are the chosen ones who we say need a second chance - or rather they are not supposed to die at that time.

When I say the right sort of person, I suppose it's very subjective, so again I feel I should let you in on a few things - explain my world a bit better.

As I've said to you I provide a service here to help people make the right decision for themselves. Not everyone comes here - perhaps only those that others - The Panel members, think perhaps deserve a second chance.

If you listen to things from The Panel's point of view they'd tell you that when the world was created it was meant to sustain only a finite number of people. And they'd tell you that the world was originally meant to be inhabited only by good people - people who would do the right things, say the right things. Now that's all well and good, and in an ideal world The Panel would have got its way, but as things progressed, well things got out of hand.

The world populated itself exponentially and The Panel just couldn't keep up.

If you look at things, Time, for example, is like any other business and as it grows it takes more and more people to look after it, and all those people need to pull in the same direction. Things start to go awry when you have people in a business making unilateral decisions that go against the main aims of the organisation - you know, sort of thinking on the hoof.

As Time passed more and more people like me were employed by The Panel to try to keep up with things - sorting good people from bad, but we've struggled over the years. I know there have been so many bad people allowed to continue their lives, just because good people don't end them for them. I am sure that if good people were allowed to take out (off) one bad person each without feeling bad about it then the world would definitely be a better place - just imagine if some right thinking,

185

good person took out, oh I don't know Genghis Khan? Pol Pot? Stalin? Hitler? - wouldn't the world have been a better place for them not being in it? Wouldn't we be sitting here now knowing that there used to be a guy called so and so, but some hero got rid of him. And why is it that only good people get assassinated? If you think back in history, and I'm talking recent history to make it easier for you, there have been so many good decent people who have been assassinated - Gandhi, Kennedy, MLK and the like - all people who whilst personally perhaps a little off, publicly did and said the right things - wanted only good things for mankind. And what happened - some lunatic, some 'bad' person decided that it was time they stopped doing that good.

Hundreds of years ago kings decided who was going to live and who was going to die - but what happened if the king was bad? It would most likely be that good people - that is to say, those opposed to him, would lose their lives.

I have been around for aeons, but I cannot take the blame for all mankind's ills. I have tried for centuries to accept what The Panel says - yes to this person, no to this one, but it's hard. I have my own opinions on who is right and who is wrong - who is bad and who is good. And if they are bad, then just how bad are they. Is there a sliding scale of right and wrong? I was going to say, who am I to judge, but, well - me actually, and that's where I am at odds with The Panel.

When a person is referred to me they arrive here and we settle them down for a couple of days - get them used to their surroundings, and in this time they hopefully become used to the fact that they need to change - or at least they have the option to change - they don't have to - as you have already seen.

I need a coffee.

I head into the diner and go behind the counter. Mike is not about, but Lorna and

Sarah are deep in conversation and keep looking over at me.

"Morning Ladies - all well in your worlds?" I ask.

"Morning Eddie" they chorus, and then laugh. They're planning something.

"What's so funny? Lorna? Sarah?"

"Oh, nothing"

"Nothing" they say almost in unison.

"You're planning something - I know you are" I challenge them.

"Eddie" begins Lorna "Can you come and sit. I have a favour to ask you".

This is trouble. Any favour she asks for will get Lorna in trouble. I'll have to be careful here, but I can't stop her.

"Sure" I say, "Let me grab my coffee".

I kicked the Rock Ola as I walked past and out came one of the best songs I've ever heard - Fleetwood Mac - You Can Go Your Own Way.

I sat, sighed, and said simply.

"Yes"

Lorna looked at me and reached across the tables to hold my hands.

"Thank you Eddie. I will come back. I promise"
"You won't Lorna. Sarah, can you give us a moment please" I asked her.
"Sure Eddie - everything OK?" Sarah looked at me.
"Yes. Fine. Give us a moment" I couldn't look at her.

As the song played, and it's only a few minutes long, I thought how to tell Lorna what she was asking was impossible for her to come back from. I had to tell her the truth. I could not lie to this sweet, wonderful girl - this child I'd saved from a wasted life, only to have her waste her life here, with me - every day the same. It wasn't fair, but the alternative was her death. Had I really just saved the memory of her grandmother for myself - a memory of the love I had lost. That wasn't fair to Lorna - like everyone else she deserved the truth and to be able to make her own decision.

"Lorna. Do you remember your mother, your grandmother?" I asked her.

"I remember my mother, but she died - drugs wasn't it? Gran died of old age probably, and maybe the shock of losing her daughter didn't help? I remember coming here from Gran's house afterwards - I remember...." she paused.

"Do you remember your sister?"

"No. I didn't know I had a sister?"

"You did. I'm sorry, but she also died, in a house fire, with her husband, all about the same time, give or take a few days. It was a local tragedy. Do you not recall that?"

"No" Lorna said, "I don't".

"Alright. But you know who I am don't you? You know the work I do here?" I queried.

"Yes Eddie. You help people - more of a wellness centre than a spa!" she joked.

"Yes. More of a wellness centre. Exactly. You clean the office don't you? You see the paperwork in my office, on my desk?"

"Yes. But Eddie. I can't read. Not a word - all that on the paper is just squiggles - mumbo jumbo to me - it could say anything".

"You can't read?" I was stunned. "Not a word?" I never knew.

"Not a word" Lorna reiterated.

"OK. How long have you been here, Lorna?"

"Ages! I don't know - two years. Three?" It was closer to twenty.

"And you still look, what? Twenty-two, twenty-three?"

191

"Oh Eddie ! I keep myself in shape - I do alright - when I'm a movie star they will give me my own creams, my own lotions - heck, I'll even do my own adverts on TV - you wait and see !"

At that moment my heart, if I had had one, should have broken. Here was this child thinking she had a future outside these surrounds, a future of glitz and glamour, whereas I knew she had never left the motel, but had woken up every morning like it was Groundhog Day - each day saving her wages in a jar for a ticket for a greyhound bus she would never take. I hated myself, but every night I emptied that jar, all bar a few dollars to give her the impression she hadn't 'quite' got enough.

I was on the verge of telling her the truth when Sarah called me over.

"Lorna, just a minute - tell you what" I said, touching her arm "Can you sort the freezer, I think it needs a defrost?"

"Sure Eddie. No problem" she got up like we hadn't even been talking and went back to the kitchen, looking around the diner as though it was the first time she'd been here.

I sat opposite Sarah, and it wasn't until she quickly withdrew her hands from the table and said what she did that I knew what I must do.

"So, Eddie, Etu. What do you say? How about you let me have my little fun with Lorna there, go on a road trip - just us girls together and then I ride off into the sunset and then we all move on?" I couldn't believe this woman was asking   me this. "And why would she want to do that, Sarah, or whatever your name is".

"Sarah, Greta, Eddie, Etu - it doesn't matter what we call ourselves does it?" she scowled "So? Road trip for us girls?"

193

"Again. Why would Lorna want to do that?"

"See the bright lights? See how the other half live? I don't know Etu, but you do have a choice. You can say no. I won't mind" Sarah wasn't right, she was not good. But I had to be sure.

"Give me a few days? Let me come to terms with it. You probably know how much she means to me?"

"Sure. A couple of days? But let me know once you've made a decision - we have plans to make….so to speak".

Chapter Fifteen

The following day I was in the reception when a strange man entered my establishment. The doorbell jangled as it normally did, the dust blew in as it normally did and the customer entered my bijou foyer, as they normally did. As the door closed it was like the air had been sucked out of the small space in front of me.

"Good morning. I was looking for a room please?" the man smiled as he spoke, placing his hands proprietorially on the desk.

" Good morning Sir, yes, let's have a look. Was it a single, a twin or a double? " I asked.

"Oh, just a single. Just for me, for two, maybe three nights?" He tilted his head.

"Certainly. A single for…let's say three nights. Now, if I can get you to complete this registration card? "I slid the paper across the desk, but something about this man made me withdraw my hand before we bumped fingers.

" Sure….but is this absolutely necessary? "

"Yes. I'm afraid so, Sir. State law. It's just a name, usual address, cell number and so on? It's not like we're asking for blood - ha!"

" Why would you say that? " The man took a step backwards, nearly ending up at the door.

"No. No. It's just a saying - you know, like, we're not asking for a lot - we're not asking for the moon, that sort of thing - really - look, just name, address and so on".

The man looked down at the card.

" Yes. But is it absolutely necessary? " He asked again.

" 'Fraid so - Dakota law being what it is. Sorry".

I wasn't sure about this man, but something made me pause. The other thing I noticed when he walked in was that the clock on the wall stopped. One second it was ticking away, and the next, it stopped - like time itself was standing still. I kept my eye on the clock, thinking I was seeing things, but no, it was stopped alright.

The man completed the card and handed it to me. I took it from him with careful fingers - 'SOMETHING'S NOT RIGHT, SOMETHING'S NOT RIGHT' my brain screamed at me, but it didn't tell me what - typical brain.

"Say, any chance of a burger? Maybe a root beer?" the man asked.

"Sure. Do you have any bags to check into your room? I can do that for you and then, as I'm the cook as well I'll have a burger sizzling before you know it" I let him know.

"No. Nothing to check in - just a rucksack - I travel light".

"Ok then. See you in the diner. Grab a table and I'll sort that burger".

The man opened the door and set off for the diner, and as he did so, the clock started up again, tick tick ticking its way around in circles.

I came out from behind the counter and picked up the card - stopping at the office I dropped it in my in-tray. My first mistake that day was letting this man stay here, the second was not taking notice of what he'd written on the card.

I got behind my counter and called across to the man.

"Hey, Mister Hanson, why don't you choose a tune on the jukebox - see if there's anything you like?"

"Sure" the man said and slid out of the booth he'd been sitting at "but call me Greg".

"OK Greg, and please, call me Eddie," I said back to him.

I knew that I knew this guy, but couldn't place him - we had met before, but I couldn't think where.

Greg went over to the Rock Ola - now here was a challenge - what would he put on. There was something dark and mysterious about this one alright, but outwardly he was all sunshine and smiles. Would he choose a light happy sing-along tune or a mean and moody one - let's see.

He stood over the jukebox a while and as I watched him I saw that he was watching me.

"Say Eddie - I keep thinking we've met? Have we?" he called over

"Yeh, I was thinking that too - hey, maybe in a former life - who knows?" I laughed

"Burger's nearly ready - fries and slaw Greg?"

"Yeh. Maybe - and yes, please to the fries and slaw" he seemed to randomly press some buttons and then sat back in the booth.

"Think your Wurlitzer's busted Eddie?" he said.

"Really - I'll take a look - it's a Rock Ola though - normally a lot more reliable than the Wurlitzer" I quipped as I placed Greg's meal and a drink on the table before him, carefully avoiding his hands.

I walked over to my beloved machine. The machine which had played hundreds of songs for me, sad songs, happy songs, and some I didn't even think were in her bulky barrel of a body. She was plugged into the wall but the lights on her normally brilliantly lit hulk were out. The usual hum of expectant readiness she had was missing and she just sat there - dark and mute. I unplugged the machine and looked at the fuse - it seemed OK. I plugged it back in and switched her on, but nothing. I couldn't work it out. She'd been working just earlier that morning. It was him. It was the clock stopper, the air taker. He'd killed my beloved Rock Ola.

"Mind if I join you Greg?" I asked.
"Erm, sure. Please do" he replied.

I slid into the booth opposite this strange man and studied him before talking.
He looked about forty, forty-five or so, and in pretty good shape, though his light brown hair had just started to thin on top. He probably weighed in at about one seventy, one eighty and was about five ten tall, but he had a mean look about him. Oh, he tried to smile it away, but I just knew, I knew, something was not right - this was not a good man.

"So, Greg. Just passing through? Business or pleasure?"

"Oh. Bit of both really. I've got to see someone I don't really want to - you know how these things are. Tie up some loose ends, but it's messy. I'm trying to put it off. But afterwards I might do a bit of sightseeing" he explained.

"Right. Yeah, I know what you mean - things can get complicated. What line of work are you in, Greg?"

"Waste management" he replied far too quickly.

"Oh right? 'Waste management' - if you watch The Sopranos you know what that means, right?"

"No? What's The Sopranos?"

"What's The Sopranos? Only the greatest mobster TV show ever - you've never seen The Sopranos Greg?" I couldn't believe it.

"No. Never heard of it. I've been out of town, away…..work related" he said.

"Hey, you'd have to have been away for a long time and been living under a rock not to have heard of that TV show".

"I have been away for a long time Eddie, but I'll certainly check it out when I get home".

"So, anyway Greg - I think we have met before, but I really can't place it - can you? Were you thinking the same thing a minute ago?" I queried.

"Yeh. I was, but perhaps I was mistaken - you know sometimes how you have a flash of a memory and then it goes? Sort of there one minute and then gone the next?"

"Sounds like me every day buddy" I said.

"Yeh. Me too. Say Eddie?"

"Yeah Greg?"

"Could I just eat my burger in peace, say, not talk maybe? I'm not much of a conversationalist really?"

"Oh. Sure. Sorry. Rude of me. I do tend to chat - I didn't mean to …."

"No. That's OK….it's just…."

"Yeah, sure, sure. I've got ……kitchen stuff….sorry".

I got up and walked back to my kitchen telling Greg if he needed anything to just call. I knew I knew him, and I think he didn't want me knowing where I'd seen him before. Not a conversationalist......didn't know The Sopranos - huh !

I cleaned up a while and kept an eye on Greg Hanson 'from Minnesota'. He ate his burger and drank his root beer without looking up and the silence was just deafening. Normally my Rock Ola would be playing - sometimes I'm sure all by itself, just quietly, like it was filling in the lack of noise, but now? Now she sat silently, and it was as if the little spirit inside her had shrunken way down in the depths of her circuitry whilst this not good man was in the house.

After what seemed an age Greg Hanson from Minnesota wiped his hands and face on a napkin, slurped the last of his drink, and getting up, nodded to me and left the diner.

I breathed a deep breath as he exited the door. That had been intense for me, and I don't normally get spooked by anyone. I think my Rock Ola felt the same for as soon as my latest guest left she also breathed and out came The Rocky Horror Show's Time Warp - I couldn't have put it better myself !

Chapter Sixteen

I now had two things to worry about. I had Lorna wanting to take a road trip, or rather the supposed Sarah, or Greta wanting to take Lorna on a road trip and now I had Greg Hanson from Minnesota staying and being weird with my electrical items - I should have told him we were full.

What to do? What to do?

I had to be careful with the Sarah / Greta situation. Mike had said he'd seen her using a compact, and in my world that meant communication - and that meant she was trouble. I contacted The Panel via a mirror and so Sarah must be contacting them as well. Sure, she could just be applying makeup, but why take any chances?
If I got rid of her and she had been talking to The Panel then I would be in serious,

deep trouble. My time here would be over, and I would have to run, and I had a good setup here - I liked it here, I didn't want to run.

If I got rid of her and she had just been applying makeup then someone would miss her - someone would come looking for her and again, things here would become very complicated.

I also had to be careful with Greg Hanson or whomever he was, as he definitely wasn't who he said he was. Oh, I know, people lie on motel forms all the time, and I have to say it didn't usually bother me - so long as they put something on them, then if asked I could say 'Oh? They seemed really genuine to me, who'd have thought?' I didn't mind what they put, but him? He was just wrong. And why did he insist on trying to nuke my clock? What had it ever done to him - and don't get me started on what he tried to do to my Rock Ola. I'd had her for so long I couldn't remember being without her, and for someone to try to fry her, well that was just monstrous, truly monstrous.

I went into the office and sought the counsel of one who knew his way around difficult situations - I sought the advice of my handyman and former hitman Mike Flanagan.

"Morning Mike. What are you up to?"
"Not a lot Eddie - just going over some paperwork. You're doing OK - you know. The casual paying guests are keeping things ticking over and the actual guests are coming quite frequently now, so Head Office will be happy".

Mike knew about The Panel, but he never said their name - he was extremely discreet for a hit man - sorry, former hitman.

"Oh, that's good Mike - glad to hear it. Say Mike? The other day? When you saw that Sarah woman?"

"Oh yeah Eddie. Good looking broad" he observed.

"Yeah. Nice looking lady I'm sure. You know you said she was using a compact?"

"Yeh"

"Using it how Mike?" I asked him.

"Err…..like a compact - you know, like broads do?"

"Like applying makeup, using - that sort of using….or?"

"Or what, Eddie? How else would a woman use a compact?"

"Well, I don't know Mike. I'm asking you".

"And I'm saying, she was using the compact, like a compact".

"OK. Right. Sorry"

"That's OK….but she was talking to herself as well , which I thought was strange".

"Talking to herself?"

"Yes. Talking to herself - and don't say - how?"

"No. OK. But……."

"Don't say it Eddie - she was just talking to herself OK".

"OK. Any idea what she was saying Mike?"

"No. No idea. Want me to keep an eye on her for you?"

"Would you?"

"My pleasure"

"And Mike?"

"Yeh Eddie?"

"Don't….you know…..don't…."

"Wouldn't dream of it".

"OK. Now. I also need you to keep an eye on another guest - a guy who's just checked in - calls himself Greg Hanson".

"But you don't think he is, right?"

"Right. He isn't"

"So why let him stay Eddie? You don't have to - you don't need the foot traffic, not all the time - you can pick and choose - it's not like you need the money" Mike also ran the rule over my books.

"I know, but it just sort of happened. I found myself there, and he was sort of there as well, and he just filled in a card?"

"Unlike   you   Eddie.   You don't normally……"

"Yeh. Get spooked by anyone, I know".

"You saw what he wrote on the card though, didn't you?"

"Not really. As I said, it just sort of happened, and I found myself dropping it in the in-tray on my way to the diner?"

"Right. Have a read of that" Mike said as he tossed a registration card over to me.

"Bastard"

"Yeh. Bastard. They're working together Eddie - you're in trouble".

There on the card was Greg's name, but it wasn't Hanson - it was Johansson - like Sarah / Greta's supposed surname. A schoolboy, or schoolgirl error - they had both used the same surname when checking in - what were the chances?

I had to tread carefully now. I couldn't make a mistake, but how would the attack come? From which direction? Would they team up? Suddenly realise they knew each other. I could imagine the conversation.

"You're not related to the Missouri Johansson's are you?" one would ask.

"Well. sort of…distantly I think" the other would answer.

" You must know Uncle Pete?' one would say.

"Yeh, Sure, old Pete, great guy" the other would say,

and there you would have it - the reason why they sat together, chatted together, heck, even went out for the day together. Plotting, planning, and scheming.

"Let me off both of them" a voice from my left brought me out of this downward reverie.

'What?"

"Let me off both of them, Eddie. Then you wouldn't have to worry"

"Mike. No. I said….don't…you know…..don't".

"Sure. When you thought it was two problems, but now? Its simpler, one problem, one solution - easy" Mike assured me.

"It's not one problem though Mike is it, well, it is, but it's a much bigger one than getting rid of two people and moving on like it never happened".

"No, it's not".

"It is Mike"

"A fire - oh yeah, a fire - that would do it…and you can claim on the insurance too. Move somewhere else, start again".

"A fire Mike. And where would I go? An insurance job would take months to sort, and I haven't got months, Lorna hasn't got months, and you haven't either come to think of it".

"Where would you go? Eddie. You do realise who you are don't you? You do realise that you could go anywhere you want….anywhere Eddie".

213

"No, I can't"

"What do you mean - you can't?"

"I can't leave Dakota".

"Yeh, you can - you did the other day - you went on that business trip - you drove - you were gone for a couple of days. Where was it you said - the meeting?"

"I said it was 'out of town' that's all 'out of town'. It wasn't anywhere. It was nowhere…..and everywhere. Mike, I just wanted to go for a drive. I just drove around".

"But you said you went to Rock Falls - with Lorna Eddie, and Rock Falls is in California - not Dakota".

"Yes I know. I risked that. I had to …to do what I did, we did".

"Risked? Why risked? What do you mean risked?"

"If I stay in Dakota then I am safe. I am on the radar, and everything is OK. If I go off the radar it's seen by The Panel, and they start asking questions - sending people….like the Johansson's - to find out

214

what I am doing - to see that things are being run properly. Do you understand?"

"So, I brought them here. I caused this danger for you?"

"No. Not at all Mike. You are here because I wanted you to be here, and ....it would be problematic for you to leave, and ...and well....you keep me company Mike, I like you - there I've said it - I need you around".

"Oh, stop it - you're making me well up. I came here looking for your help - you didn't ask me to come here".

"You really don't remember how you came to be here Mike do you? You don't know why you came to Dakota - why you were in my little area of control?"

"What? Yes, of course I do....the cheap gas...I was driving by and saw the cheap gas"

"You're telling me that cheap gas brought you here - where were you before that - before the lure of petroleum brought you to my doorstep Mike? Where were you driving from? Can you remember?"

"Well, no, probably not. It's a long time ago – ten years isn't it? A guy can forget a lot in ten years''.

"Shall I tell you? I remember everything. I have to, it's my job. Shall I tell you Mike?"

"OK. Please. Tell me. It feels like you want to".

"I don't Mike, that's the point. I don't want to remind you why you came here, specifically. But as you don't know, I will tell you. Please sit, let's have a coffee".

I grabbed us a pot and brought it back to the table. Supposed Sarah and supposed Greg were elsewhere and at the moment I was too tired to bother wondering where that elsewhere was, and what they were planning.

"Mike. As you told me, you came from Ireland and carried out many jobs for the bookmaker whilst settling into your new life in America. You were, as you do remember, a hired hit man, doing his work for many years until you called time on it all. The reason, as you know now, that people mainly come here is that they are dead, but that they are thought to deserve another chance. I know that we get casual live customers and that they stay whilst they rest a while, but for the main part dead people walk through the door. So….Mike….think back to when you came here".

"I was dead".

"Correct Mike. You were dead. You were not 'on your way' to anywhere else, you were not 'passing through and saw cheap gas'. You died in my area and, as it turns out, a clerical error brought you here - that's all."

"Are you saying I was a mistake?"

"No. Mike. A clerical error. Someone somewhere made a clerical error. And…due to that clerical error you've enjoyed another ten years of life. Now that's the sort of error I think everyone would love to have made for them, don't you?"

"So…"

"So, a clerical error was made and at the point of your death, your timeline was wiped by The Panel….but you still landed here".

"Why would I land here then? Why here specifically?"

"Because. I saw the error. I was sitting in my office at the time when I was notified of your death, but then the timeline was wiped, and it was sent as an error report. But you had already landed here - in my catchment area. And at a good time….for both of us"

"Why was I in Dakota then Eddie? Why was I in your 'catchment area'?"

"Erm…you may think you died whilst carrying out a job for the bookmaker. But it's complicated. You were sort of doing me a favour as it turned out, and so, when I saw your name on the computer, purely by chance I thought you deserved a bit more time".

"I don't understand. What was the job?"

"Well, it's interesting that you said a fire, here, to resolve my situation…as you were actually killed in a fire - one that you set yourself?

"Oh? I don't remember".

"No. I made sure that you didn't. That's not the sort of thing one would want to remember - so I sort of wiped it for you".

"Thanks. Appreciated. Who was I torching - I do recall having a liking for a fire"

"You set fire to a man's house. At the time it had him and his wife in it"

"And I take it the guy was the target?"

"Yes. They were asleep, but in different rooms - they were having ….erm…marital difficulties. He was on the couch, in the front room, and she, as it turns out was upstairs, in a back bedroom".

"Hang on…old guy?….real old guy? - I do remember….but not why I was doing the hit?"

"It wasn't the bookmaker that asked you to do it Mike, it was me".

"So, who was the old guy?"

"It was Lorna's real grandfather. He'd returned to Dakota. I couldn't believe it. So many years after up and leaving Estelle - he just came back. Settled down with another woman like he'd never been away, and I couldn't let that happen Mike, I really couldn't…so I sort of moved things around…I sort of made his timeline a little shorter…a little harsher for him….."

"Harsher…..? He fried Eddie. He fried along with plastic and foam - Jesus".

"Oh, I'm sorry Mike, how do people normally die in fires - I feel bad enough as it was that his wife died - fortunately she'd taken enough pills to knock out a herd of elephants, but go on, tell me, how do people normally die nicely in fires ?"

"When I'm doing them, they die and then they go up in a fire - I used to shoot them - less pain. No malice, just doing my job".

"Ah. OK. I see, sorry. Yes. I suppose there was malice as you say in wanting him to die horribly.

Suddenly Lorna ran into the diner.

"Eddie, come quick, Tommy's woken up…..and he's…not good".

Chapter Seventeen

The three of us raced to Tommy's room - it was, fortunately at the far end of the lot for, as when we entered number 20 he was writhing on the bed and foaming at the mouth, screaming, and shouting obscenities that would make even the most hardened sailor blush.

"Gag him" I said to Lorna.
"What? Eddie? No, he's choking" she replied.
"No. He's not. He's fine - this is how he wakes up when he's been out for a while. Clean him up and then gag him. I need to think, and I don't need the Johansson's coming and seeing who we've got and wanting to help out."

Lorna did as I asked whilst I paced up and down, up and down outside. Tommy had been like this before, had awoken screaming and shouting. I don't know what he expected - wherever he went, whatever he did, he never came back in a better state than when he left - it was like he was trying to kill himself, but always making a bad job of it.

As you know Tommy Zeitz was our star guest and I was supposed to give him the star treatment. But it was hard - Tommy made it difficult for me and my unofficial staff. You see the thing that Tommy had was money and money spoke to The Panel. Tommy had paid The Panel an awful lot of money for a special plan. The normal plans I dealt with allowed people to effectively trade some years for a chance to go back and redo or undo the things that had caused them trouble - usually ending in their deaths.

Most people grabbed this opportunity with both hands, rarely reading the small print of the paperwork I put in front of them - why should they care what the future held when they were trying to resolve the past and the present. I could understand that I knew how they felt to have made a mess of things in one's past, and so the chance to change things for the better was usually one too good to pass up for most people.

But Tommy had paid for an extra special plan - he was allowed to go back, and relive the past, and although he was supposed to be putting things right, he never did. He just kept making the same mistakes as he always did - the drink, the drugs, the women. If he hadn't suffered the injury he did when he did, then something else horrific would have happened to him - some people are just ticking timebombs. The Tommy Zeitz's of this world attract trouble and there is nothing you, me, or any amount of money can do to stop them falling into it. I don't know why The Panel took his money like they did - people like us didn't need money - we had no real use for it, but they took it, and well, here we are. Or rather, here I am, having to placate Tommy Zeitz and mollycoddle him every time he crossed my doorstep.

As I walked up and down in the parking lot I thought of the first time Tommy had come here. He had died due to an overdose but someone, somewhere had sent word to me that he was coming my way. I didn't like it and I said so - I made my feelings loud and clear, but no-one listened. I said that we should not be pandering to people with money, and that people who decide to party too hard and take as many drugs as they could in an evening deserved exactly what they got. No-one listened.

I paused things for him when he arrived - like his timeline. I asked him to take a seat and I would be with him shortly. I then spent the next few hours being put on hold, being cut off, being passed to answer machines. The Panel had spoken, or rather they had not. By their silence they had told me what I was supposed to do, and so I begrudgingly started Tommy up again.

"So, hello. Welcome to my humble establishment" I began.

"Yeh, hi. I don't know why I'm here. I should be at my hotel, not this dump" he slouched on my counter as he slurred his introduction to me.

"And a jolly good afternoon to you as well Sir. Welcome to my humble, and drug free establishment. If you'd like to take a seat before you fall over?"

"Yeh. Whatever. Look. There's obviously been some mistake. I was told I would be taken care of. I was told I would be treated well - look, is your boss about? Let me speak to someone in charge".

"I am the boss, and I am more in charge than you know".

"I doubt it, guy. Look, here's a ten - go get me a beer would you?"

"No"

"What? What did you say?"

"Oh. I'm sorry - try this - NO ! Sit down, shut up. Fill this in" I said as I threw him a registration card.

"Why should I? Don't you know who I am?"

"Oh. I know who you are alright. But do you know who I am?" I could be menacing if I wanted to be "If you knew who I was - what I could do to you - you wouldn't be so…so…." I breathed. And restarted.

"Now. Mr Zeitz, if you would be so very kind as to complete the card in your hand, and then follow me to the diner, I will see if we can't find you that beer. How's that?"

"That's more like it. A little more service like"

"You need to mind your step".

"What? What did you say to me" Tommy said as he fell out of the foyer

"Mind the step - never mind. Are you OK? This way please"

Tommy picked himself up, dusted off his trousers and walked, or rather shuffled along beside me. I opened the diner door and led him to a table.

I handed him a menu and offered to cook him something but the way he looked briefly at the options and set the menu down told me he wasn't going to eat anything.

"You'll need to eat Mr Zeitz".

"Nah. I'll leave it thanks. Got that beer?"

"Certainly. But I would urge you to eat something. You may be away for a couple of days and the body does need sustenance even when its asleep, I assure you".

"And I assure you......whatever your name is, that my little friend here will keep me going just fine" he said as he withdrew a bag of white powder from his inside pocket.

I let him open the seal on the bag, I let him tap out a small amount of the powder onto my Formica table, I let him use an Amex gold card to make a line, and just as he bent to snort it I punched him fully to the side of the head with as much force as I could muster from a standing start. He flew across the booth ending up slamming into the wall. The powder flew from the table and as I ground it into the floor I bent over the former football player, the former playboy, the former TV host and whispered.

"Don't forget who will be looking over you while you sleep. Now, how about some food, young man?"

A little while later a quieter Tommy Zeitz approached me at the counter.

"Say….thanks for the food - it was actually OK. I'm sorry about earlier. I think it was the drugs - you know, lack of…ha ! No. honestly, I am sorry - look, here's a twenty for your trouble. Can we start again? Can we be friends?"

"Thank you Mr Zeitz for your words. Please keep your money - it is of no use here. No, we cannot be friends. I am performing a service for you here, nothing more. I did not ask you to come here, in fact I requested that you be allowed to continue on your own particular journey, one of self-destruction it would seem, but higher powers than I have spoken, and well....here we are".

"Oh"

"Oh indeed. I mean no offence, and whilst you are here I will do what I can to accommodate you, but please - do as I say, without question...without ...attitude, and we will get along fine. Do I make myself clear?"

"Sure"

I wondered for a while why Tommy had so readily backed down. He suddenly seemed like a broken man, one who would do exactly what I said. Something had happened. Something had made him come to his senses. Made him think of his position? I couldn't think what it was. I knew I had lost my temper earlier - it was the drugs on my table, in my diner - I would not have that. The sight of it had made me see red as the saying goes, but what had my reaction made Tommy see? I went to the office to see Mike.

Mike listened to what I said. He nodded and assured me that everything would be well. He would sort things. He offered then and there to get rid of Tommy Zeitz for me, but I said no. I told Mike that Tommy Zeitz was protected, I could not make a decision of my own regarding this particular guest. Whilst we had been talking Mike had been winding back the CCTV that I kept running 24/7 in the diner

"Oh, shit Eddie" he suddenly exclaimed.
"What?" I asked, "what is it?"
"Hey. No wonder he backed down - you are a scary dude when you want to be. Remind me never to upset you".

"I know I shouted at him; I know I punched him - that's all" I was sure.

"Well. Something did, but it wasn't you Eddie".

I looked at the image that Mike had frozen on the screen.

And there I was, in all my glory.

"Oh shit" I said.

Chapter Eighteen

Now, Weary Traveller, I've had Mike wipe that CCTV, no-one needs to see what we saw - my actual image.

I let myself get agitated, I let Tommy Zeitz get under my skin, and I shouldn't have. It doesn't happen often thankfully, but sometimes I do let my guard down and well, the real me comes out. I'm not scary when that happens, I'm just different.

Perhaps if I told you from a beginning - not *the* beginning, but *a* beginning. I've been telling you bits and pieces of my story and trying to convince you that I really am a nice guy - and I am, but we all have a history. We all have a back story we're trying to get away from, cover up - it's just that mine is a little….different from most peoples.

I won't go back a long way, maybe just less than a couple of hundred years or so…..oh? You seem surprised? I told you I was old - I know I look younger in a good light, but I am actually ancient. Not like that old, 'ancient' relative everyone has that turns up at every family event and drinks all the sherry, but actually ancient. I've been around for an awfully long time and have seen things no one person should have to see - but, well, that's the nature of the job I have, so there's no point complaining.

My current guise is that of a mild-mannered motel owner called Eddie, and it's OK I really am not a hit man, but my real name is Etu. You see Etu is the name the Lakota people of Dakota - the original settlers in this area, gave to Time itself. I am; therefore, many would say, the personification of Time. And to be honest it's a lot of pressure for one person. For longer than I care to remember I have had to work for The Panel on their overall plan for mankind and make decisions based on their view of things.

I've gone along with what they say because often it's easier than to keep challenging them, but sometimes you have to make a stand, and from time to time I have made that stand. It hasn't always done me good - The Panel have long memories and as they never forget to point out - I work for them, not the other way around. I'll give you an example.

As I say, I have to go back a while - nearly a couple of hundred years ago, someone came to me, no leaflets then, just word of mouth.

At that time, I travelled with the Lakota people, it seemed right, and I pretended to be a shaman, it was easier than explaining to everyone who I actually was and as their beliefs were rooted in time it was easier to be the person who they thought I was rather than tell them the truth. I didn't feel right lying to my own people, but the truth would have been so much worse. They wouldn't have believed me, they would have killed me, or, worse, shunned me, which to be honest would have been the end for me.

We roamed the land looking for good sites to set up, to hunt, to settle on and so on, and from time to time we did stay all in one place for long spells.

It was the time when the white man decided he wanted to settle as well, and as you know from your history things got very messy when he chose our lands.

Now, I am obviously biased and would say that before the white man came we were a calm, peaceful group of nations. I accept that we had a few differences between us and that those differences were normally settled with the in-fighting and slaughter of hundreds of our own people, but apart from that we were peaceful. We fought between ourselves and usually agreed afterwards to move on and to go our own separate ways, each accepting the differences between our tribes.

But the white man brought us one thing. The white man brought us unity. He showed us a common enemy - the enemy who believed he had a right to our lands. Arrogance is not a thing the Lakota tolerate - perhaps that's why I reacted to Tommy as I did. Maybe I saw that arrogance - that total disregard for another human being - who knows?

Over the next number of years, we fought long and hard with the white man and won many battles against him, but their numbers were greater than ours, and their firepower was too much for us, and so one by one the tribes submitted to the inevitable - they gave way to the white man's strength and moved to reservations, to camps where they were counted and treated like cattle.

But some resisted. Some, like the man I will tell you about, believed if he could talk to the white man, if he could make him see the error of his ways then we could live alongside each other peacefully.

At this time, we had been resisting the white man in the form of American soldiers. There had been much bloodshed on both sides, and he wanted no more of it.

This man came to see me - his shaman and told me that he had had a dream. In his dream he had seen many soldiers, as thick as grasshoppers falling into the Lakota camp. This he and his people believed was a foreshadowing of a major victory. But the man knew that even if he won such a victory for his people the white man would still eventually overpower him.

I advised the man. I told him that the white man would not hear him, that they would kill him if he went to them. He was not surrendering and anything else they would see as rebellion and deal with it accordingly.

But he would not listen. He thanked me for my counsel but said that he must try. He felt it was the only way to save more senseless slaughter.

I understand that the man went to the white man's camp. He spoke to the one they called Yellow Hair, but who you know better by another name.

The man spoke at length and tried to convince the white man that no one could win. No one could come away from their position with any honour.

Yellow Hair would not listen. He told the Lakota leader that he had his orders, and those orders were that every last Native American must surrender or be killed.

And so, one of the most avoidable battles in the history of America was fought and many people were slaughtered. The Lakota peoples claimed a great victory at the Battle of The Little Bighorn but at a great cost to them, as subsequently they were besieged by more white men than they knew existed and those who were not slaughtered and did not escape were rounded up and sent to reservations to live out their lives like cattle.

My leader - whom I knew by another name, but who you would recognise as

Sitting Bull, escaped, and much to his shame led a small band of followers North where they lived like nomads until they surrendered rather than freeze to death.

My leader, my friend, was killed some years later by soldiers who believed he was trying to lead a revolt against them.

I tell you all this as when he came to me, I wanted to give him a second chance, I had a plan worked out for him, but The Panel refused. They said that he should be allowed to die, that history would be his honour and that as a Native American he would be remembered as a true hero, and a warrior against oppression.

I tried to argue but was told no. Sitting Bull was a good man, but The Panel had history to think about, they said. Things had a way of working themselves out they said and that in time I would see that they were right. And so, this good man died, and I am still waiting to see the right in what they said.

I tell you all of this as it will explain to you why I stay where I am, why I stay in Dakota. I am Dakota. I am Time in this area and were I to leave then I would not be. I do not know what would happen to me if I were to leave Dakota but everything that I have built up, everything that I have fought for would be lost.

I know that were I to leave then The Panel would track me down. They would hunt me like the white man hunted the Lakota, across the plains and into the frozen North. I would be no better off than my friend I told you about.

Maybe The Panel have already started to hunt me, but in a different way. They have sent one of the Johansson's as a scout - which is what the white man did. They send one person to see how things lie - to report back and then make their plans. Well. No more. I will take the high ground. I will be on the front foot. I refuse to sit back and await the end that I know is inevitable.

Chapter Nineteen

It had been two days since I spoke to Sarah, when I'd asked her for time to make my decision about Lorna. Strange that I, Time itself, asked someone else for time. I could have stopped the woman's timeline, I could have removed her from here, from everywhere, but if she was a scout for The Panel they would then know, they would then be alerted to my knowledge, my resistance, and I needed to be careful if my plan was to succeed.

I had now made my decision. I had decided to tell Lorna the truth and let her make her own choice. After all I have said about people choosing their own paths, their own journeys, I have been somewhat hypocritical in stopping Lorna from choosing her own fate, her own destiny. I'd brought her here as a favour to her mother, giving her more time than she had, but had

I done it purely for her, to give her more time? Or had I done it for me, and my own selfish reasons?

Lorna had lived a day-to-day existence here but had not had a life as such. She had not been past the confines of the motel or diner for years - and since I reset her timeline each night she knew nothing of the outside world. I must be honest with her and set her free.

I was in the diner and as I had not had any guests for a few days, either passing or staying we were quite quiet.

I currently had Larry and Tommy in rooms and would have to deal with them when I got a minute, but for the moment my most pressing thing was doing the right thing by Lorna.

"Say, Lorna - got a minute?" I called down the kitchen.

"Sure Eddie, what's up?" She was just a child. How could I have treated her so badly, by trying to treat her so well. She was all innocence but felt she could take on the world. It would eat her alive if it got to her. It wasn't fair, either way, it just wasn't fair.

"Take a seat. I need to speak to you" I began.

"Again? What's this Eddie? You're so serious today" she smiled that girlish smile.

"Should have seen me yesterday" I said.

"I did….didn't I?" she looked puzzled.

"Look, Lorna. I need to talk to you, to tell you the truth. To let you decide what you want to do" I was flustered. I didn't know how to tell her, but I knew I must.

"Well then Eddie. Why not just take a breath and start. What truth? What's bothering you ?"

"OK. You came here, with me a while ago now and well, I've sort of kept you here - no - I've encouraged you to stay…the truth…the truth….I've been making you stay here. Maybe not against your will, I've not kidnapped you, just sort of…well,

244

made you think that you want to be here"

"But I do want to be here Eddie - this is where I work, where I live".

"See. I've done a good job on you"

"No you haven't Eddie. I choose to be here. Honestly"

"No Lorna, you don't - I make you be here. Each night I….I"

"Empty the tips jar - yes I know".

"What…?"

"You empty the tips jar and make me think that I've 'nearly got enough' to buy a bus ticket outta here".

"How…?"

"You tell me every night to forget what has happened that day and I think that you think I'm sort of reset in the morning? Is that about right Eddie?"

"Yes, but how did you know? How can you know - I reset you…I?"

"Eddie. You probably did for the first few weeks? Months? Years? I don't know, but these past few weeks you've taken your eye off the ball - you've seemed distracted and so when you started to talk to me in the evening, I sort of stopped listening. I started singing songs to myself, and so your words had less effect on me, and I focussed on the songs, not you. You've been busy - I know, and I don't blame you. You've been trying to protect me, and that's sweet, but you don't need to. I can look after myself - you don't need to do that anymore. I will be OK".

"Oh?. But all I wanted was for you to be happy. I was doing it for you".

"If you say so Eddie. But I am happy here. I'll do whatever you want to stay happy - to keep you happy".

"But don't you want to leave Lorna, don't you want to explore the outside world?"

"Sure, maybe, one day - who knows - perhaps when my tip jar is full".

"So, a road trip with Sarah? Is that something you want to do? Go outside - explore?"

"God no. She's a whacko. I've seen her talking to herself. She thinks I don't see her.

She doesn't wear any makeup at all, yet she's always using that compact and talk talk talk. It's like she's talking to the thing". "OK. Decision made then. You do exactly what you want, but can I suggest something to you, sort of a 'you help me, and I'll help you' kind of thing?"

"Sure. But I have a plan as well Eddie - not like your types of plan, but a much simpler one. Let me talk to her".

It was some days later that I next saw Lorna. She had gone on a road trip with Sarah and though I knew what would happen to her I had had to let her go. I had seen her in deep conversation with Sarah over a beer one evening and the next morning both were gone.

I had been in the office when Mike ran in

"Quick Eddie. You need to come... its Lorna".

We both ran to the reception where, had I not seen it myself I would not have believed it. There, standing in my foyer was a middle-aged woman, she looked a bit like Lorna, but older. This wasn't Lorna surely.

"Hello? Can I help you?" I asked the woman.

"Eddie. It's me - Lorna - don't you recognise me?" she said as she took off her sunglasses. It was her but she seemed to have aged about thirty years.

"Lorna? My God? I thought…?" I stammered.

"Shall I complete a card Eddie? Shall I….." and then she collapsed to the floor.

Mike and I picked her up and took her quickly to a room - she needed rest and I needed to think. We laid her on the bed and took off her shoes. Her legs and feet were covered in dirt and her skirt was ripped and just as filthy - what on earth had happened to this poor girl?

Lorna lay there for a day and a night, not moving, not speaking - for all intents and purposes she was in a deep sleep, or worse.

Finally, after sitting by her side for the longest time, I was rewarded when she awoke and asking for a drink of water she propped herself up on her elbow.

"Have I got a story for you Eddie" she croaked.

"Slowly, then Lorna. In your own time, and then we'll work out a plan for you" I told her.

"No. It's OK Eddie. I don't need a plan. I'm happy. I'm back here again, where I belong, but let me tell you what happened. I've been gone so long".

I couldn't tell her she had only been gone a few days.

"So, Sarah and I went on that road trip. She said she had always wanted to do it, and that I was the one she wanted to go with. Kinda weird, I thought, - we'd only just met and so the alarm bells were ringing, but I thought I'd go along with it".

"But why did you go at all?"

"My story - my telling it. Just listen"

"Sorry"

"So, we set off in her Coupe - lovely car - a shame what happened to it…."

"Dare I?"

"No, you dare not. So, there we are in her Coupe, running along at a steady seventy when she asks me, where did I want to go. So, I said, I had no idea, I'd not been out and about for a while and so I didn't mind where we went. Sarah said we should go to California…"

"Don't tell me - Rock Falls?"

"Yes. How did you know?"

"Please. Do go on".

"She said she had something to do there, something that had been waiting a while and so I said sure, fine, let's take a detour. So, we went to California. When we got there we parked up and then walked along a track. She had an urn with her, and she said it was…."

"Her husband?"

"Yeh. Her husband. So, we walked along this track until we came to a clifftop. She said that she and her husband had been together for a long time and that she would really miss him. She said that she'd come a long way to be here but had to let him go - which was really sad".

"Lorna….did you….?"

"I did, yes. I thought it's really sad that two people so obviously in love as she continually told me they were should ever be parted, and so when she had her eyes closed and was talking to him I sort of nudged her….sort of shoved her…well OK - I ran at her and hit her hard, and over the edge she went".

"Oh Lorna" I said.

"It's OK Eddie - she had her husband with her. It all happened so quickly, but I did right didn't I? I did the right thing - she was a   bad   person   wasn't   she?"
"Yes. She was a bad person".
"And then I climbed down the cliff, I had to make sure - to see that she was gone - as in…."
"Ah. I wondered why you were so scuffed up".
"Yeah. Eddie. But I sort of need a favour…again…."
"How so?"
"Well. She was obviously a bad person. The moment I saw her here I knew she was looking to cause trouble and that's why I was happy to go with her, to finish her off. But to make sure, I lay at the bottom of that cliff with her for a day, making sure she didn't get up, making sure she really was dead. When I was sure I climbed up the hill and jumped in her car, but as I was driving back I started to feel so tired, like I'd never

been before, and I got the shock of my life when I looked in the mirror".

"You'd started to age?"

"Yes. No more face cream adverts for me then huh?"

"No, probably not - so what happened to the car".

"I torched it a way down the road" Mike said.

"What?" I asked, "You knew about this Mike?"

"No. I didn't know that Lorna had gone anywhere until yesterday, and it wasn't until she called me earlier today to come and get her that I knew for sure that she'd gone anywhere. She was in such a state Eddie - you need to help her".

"How can I help you Lorna - you're not dead. I can't offer you a plan - there isn't anything that fits".

"I want to come back here Eddie. I've seen the outside world and it's not for me anymore. I want to come back here. If I can stay here, always here, you can keep taking

253

the tip money out of the jar, keep resetting me in the evening - like before. I won't leave again - I promise".

"That's no life Lorna - that can't be all you want, surely?"

"There is no one out there for me - it's all changed Eddie - it's not what it used to be. I'm happy here - please, let me stay".

"Alright. Alright. Let me think. There is a way, but it's a once done, always done sort of thing".

"I'll take it".

"Wait…..please wait…..you will always be as you are now - there will be no coming back from that - you will live each day like the previous one, for all time".

"I'll take it".

"Think…please…don't just say 'I'll take it'...please. You will be like me - seeing people you love pass on, seeing those who came before you, age and die while you watch - please Lorna - it is not the answer. It is not the answer for me and I'm sure it's not the answer for you either".

"I will be eternal Eddie - I will not age, I will not die - please let me have that. All I want is here, in this motel, in this small world, it is all I need".

"Lorna. I need to think. I can make that happen, but it cannot be what you want. Sleep on it. Think about it for a couple of days. There is someone for everyone - you need to get out there, you need to explore - like you said only the other day - you need to…to be".

"No Eddie. I know I do not. I am too naive to survive, I cannot spend each day looking over my shoulder, wondering if people are taking me for a ride, just because I'm nice, just because I trust too easily. All my life I've trusted and look where it's got me - I fell for the first man who showed me any sort of attention and look who that was - no, I've made up my mind."

Chapter Twenty

While I left Lorna to rest and to think about what she wanted to do I had two guests to attend to.

After I had spoken to Larry he had said that he wanted to go back, to try and save the Mannerheim's from dying. They had been his trusting clients and he had abused that trust. He wanted to do right by them, he wanted to go back and
right his wrong.

Unfortunately, though for Larry he had very little time left - he was not aware, but when he had jumped off the roof of his building due to guilt he was actually saving himself from a world of pain. Oh, he would feel the pain of a concrete pavement impacting on him at lightning speed - or rather him impacting on it, but the pain he would have suffered had he survived the fall would have been so much worse. Larry had terminal cancer, but he just didn't know it yet and no amount of pain-killing drugs or treatment would have saved him - I estimated he had about six months to live, and those months would be consumed with pain and agony he did not deserve.

I had left Larry in a room and whilst he was lying down and was calm I could not say if he had slept, and if he had it would only have been fitfully. He was in torment from what he had done, and my kind words would not help him, any plan I had would be pointless for him, but I thought I should try - give him an alternative. I shook him lightly awake and spoke to him softly.

"Hello Larry, here have a drink - you've been out for a long time".
"Thanks Eddie - I do feel a little better, but am I alive? Did I go back - are they alive?"
"The Mannerheim's? - No. Not yet. Is that what you want Larry - to save them?"

257

"Yes. Yes. Of course - I would do anything, anything to save them - Oh God, nothing's changed - I thought I would wake up and everything would be better"

"No. Not yet - but I have a plan - not a plan as is described in our leaflets but a plan nevertheless - did you want to hear it?"

"Yes Eddie - please tell me - I will do anything".

"Ok. Stay here a moment".

For the next part of this particular plan, I needed the help of my handyman and having found him fixing a roof I asked him to bring some rope and follow me.

We then went to room 20 and woke the sleeping beauty there.

"Morning Tommy - how are you on this fine day?" I asked.

"What...? What are you...? Why am I tied to the bed?"

"Oh, you're not tied to the bed Tommy. You are tied up I accept, but you are actually chained to the bed - now - listen to me I have a little favour to ask of you".

I then told Tommy my plan for him - at first he was not happy - he said he saw no reason why he should help someone else and didn't have to do anything he didn't want to. Let's just say that I encouraged him to see my point of view - I advised him with careful words that if he did not comply then things would get increasingly uncomfortable for him and that my historic ways may come to the fore once more, and I knew that he did not like seeing my original form.

After my little pep talk I am sure that Tommy said he would willingly help the person, though he hoped to be better off at the end of the day. I assured him he would be better off than he was now, which seemed to convince him.

Mike and I then moved Tommy from his room to the one next door.

"Larry, this is Tommy - Tommy - Larry".

"Hi" Larry said.

"Yeh, can't shake your hand at the moment man" Tommy smirked.

"Thanks for doing this Tommy - I appreciate it".

"Doing what? Hey, wait a minute - I was told I was swapping places with someone - what is all this? I'm happy to help you Barry, but no offence, you don't seem as advertised".

"It's Larry - and I am actually a very rich commodities broker I'll have you know - and you are…..hey, wait a minute - you're Tommy Zeitz."

"Guilty"

"Of many things guy" said Mike "Shall we get on?"

"Tommy Zeitz? - I'm swapping places with Tommy Zeitz. How?"

"Wait a minute - swapping places with him? I don't know anything about …what did you call them..?"

"Commodities - think of them as just things Timmy".

"Tommy"

"Yeah. I'm ready when you are Eddie" Larry said as he lay back on the bed.

Mike and I sat Tommy on the chair and made sure he was secure. I would not say that he was ready or prepared, but he was secure.

Now, what happened is a bit of a trade secret so I cannot go into details but at the start of my story I asked what someone would give to trade places with someone else, to live their life for even a day?

Well Larry was prepared to give everything. I had explained to him that he had very little time left and that his choices were extremely limited. It obviously came as a shock to him, but he chose wisely in my opinion.

You see I think Larry was a good person at heart and whilst he....well let's come to that later - let's talk about Larry first.

Larry chose Tommy Zeitz's life over death. Tommy Zeitz - the washed-up pro footballer, full of drugs and alcohol and so shot to pieces that he really should not be alive at all. The man was so full of arrogance and disdain towards others that he deserved nothing from anyone.

For Larry to choose to 'be' Tommy Zeitz and live his life with all that it held was a poor second choice - but the alternative was death. If Larry had made any other choice he would have died and so on he went, just in a different guise.

I knew I was taking a risk and that The Panel would eventually find out, but I had to rewind a number of timelines about six months. I understand that 'Tommy Zeitz' made a full recovery from his various addictions and that his 'treatment centre' was considered one of the best in the world.

It also transpired that the Mannerheim's had not shot themselves - they were apparently on the point of bankruptcy and the rumours were that they were 'suicidal', but at the last moment an anonymous but significant donation was made to them and saved them from making a terrible and final choice. They now live quietly overseas and have given away an awful lot of their money to various charities.

'Tommy Zeitz' now also lives quietly and lectures on the dangers of drug and alcohol addiction - in what was held to be one of the most remarkable turnarounds in someone's life he is held up as a role model for many young men and women across America.

Unfortunately, the real Tommy Zeitz - the now 'Larry' was not so lucky. Whilst the former Larry had done the right thing for himself and many others, what the new 'Larry' woke up to was a falling sensation.

Well, in truth it was more than a sensation - it was a feeling, and a feeling that grew increasingly windier the longer it went on….until it didn't.

The papers told the story of a commodities broker who had gambled and drunk and smoked his life away. They told of a sad story that things came to a head for the young man when the markets crashed and he could no longer cover his losses, deciding then and there to leap from the roof of the building to his death.

Was Tommy Zeitz MkI a bad person - yes. He was. He had lived a life which was full of promise and had so many opportunities to do the right thing - but what started him on a bad path? Was it being benched too many times, was it the bad injury, who knows. Certainly, after then it went rapidly downhill for him but even so players get injured all the time. Many come back and make a good living in other areas of the game and life generally. Some do go off the rails and we feel somehow sorry for them, and they are not bad people, just people gone wrong. Tommy Zeitz was bad though - he had the opportunities to help others, to use his position and his wealth for good, but did not.

I often ask myself though, was Larry MkI a good person? Was he any better than Tommy Zeitz? Was he a good person gone wrong and a Tommy bad one from the start? Was it that simple? Probably not. Larry had gone astray, massively astray but had felt guilt, and so much so that he had leapt to what he thought was his own death.

And it was not me who had saved him, had given Larry a second chance - it was The Panel, so maybe they had seen the good still in him - perhaps I should ask them…or perhaps I shouldn't.

Chapter Twenty-One

The day started well in that the music was on - volume full up, as I was on my own in the diner - Wake Me Up ! - by Wham, blasting out on all speakers - it really was a sound to behold and it was so loud that I didn't hear the door open and close, and nor did I hear or see, the supposed Greg Hanson sidle, no, creep, no, slime, up to my counter.

I was in the kitchen with a wooden spoon in hand as my microphone and dancing old man style to the dulcet tones of Andrew and George - (the wrong one went too soon in my opinion) when the music suddenly stopped, and I saw the air thief sitting there. Again? Leave my Rock Ola alone!

"Greg. How you doing? Did you unplug my jukebox or just look at it?"

"Sorry?"

"Did you walk past it and pull the plug out by any chance?"

"No. I didn't Eddie, why would I do that?"

"Lord alone knows - never mind - what can I get you Greg?"

"Just wondered about a Dakota special?"

"Really? Sure. On its way - take a seat and I'll bring it to you when it's ready"

"Thanks Eddie, appreciate it".

A few minutes later I plated up the enormous breakfast and on Lorna's silver tray took it over to the diner's solitary customer.

"No Lorna today Eddie?" Greg asked.

"No. She's feeling a little poorly - having a lie in I think" I replied.

"Shame - seems like a nice girl".

"Yeah, she is. Anything else I can get you Greg? Coffee? Tea?" I asked him.

"Oh, coffee please, if it's not too much trouble?"

"OK - coffee it is. No trouble at all" - why was he being so nice all of a sudden - making small talk now as well.

Maybe Greg Hanson from Minnesota, or Missouri or wherever had heard from The Panel that Sarah had had an unfortunate accident. Maybe he felt a little exposed and outnumbered all of a sudden, and was biding his time, being nice….or maybe I had totally misjudged him. Maybe he was actually who he said he was, and I was just being paranoid about him. I'd let Mike keep an eye on him and see where it went.

Whilst Greg ate in silence I busied myself in the kitchen and thought how I could resolve my situation.

I needed to get out. I couldn't stay here anymore. Too many things had happened and too many roads led straight back to me.

I had been honest with Mike - if I left Dakota I would not be Etu anymore, anything I had going on would be lost and I would just be plain old Eddie.

But at the moment that sounded pretty good to me - imagine the freedom I could have being just plain old Eddie - no Head Office chasing me for targets, no talking poor saps into plans they really didn't want just to keep the figures up, no responsibilities. What a wonderful thought - I could just walk away.

There was a knock on the rear kitchen door and when I answered it I saw Mike standing there with a smile on his face.

"Morning Boss. All good in your world?" he asked.

"Yeah, all good Mike - what are you smirking at?"

"Have you noticed our Mr Hanson is looking a bit stubbly this morning?"

"No, not really - why what have you done?"

"Nothing really - just taken away his mirror - well all of his mirrors - he's a sneaky one - he had one in his rucksack and one taped to the underneath of the bedside cabinet drawer - sort of his emergency one I guess".

"And where are they now Mike?"

"Never you mind Eddie - they are safe and won't be used by the clock stopper"

"Oh, you heard about that?"

"Yeah. I could stop his clock if you wanted - you understand me?"

"Sure Mike. I understand you, but then The Panel would come looking - two scouts lost while poking around here? It would look too suspicious".

"Everything OK Boss?" Mike asked me.

"Yes. I think so Mike. I'm thinking of going away for a while though".

"Oh? Another meeting?"

"No. Going away, away. Leaving. Starting over somewhere else"

"Oh? I just sort of thought you'd go on - you know for good?"

"No. I don't think anyone just goes on forever - not if they truly want to be free".

"Woh….too deep for me. Lorna said she wanted to go on forever - will you let her? Will you do that for her?"

"I will, if that's what she really wants, but it's not all it seems Mike - it honestly isn't. I've seen so many people I got attached to, go on before me and it does get kinda lonely".

"Yeah. I can imagine. So, what did you want? What did you see yourself doing?"

"Well first. I want to travel. I want to see all the sights that other people see - with my own eyes - not through theirs. I want to go places and be like a real person. And I want to get away from The Panel, but I know that I can't".

"But what if you could?"

"I couldn't"

"But what if you could - what if we could?"

"Mike, you know that if I stay in Dakota The Panel will see me, they will find me

and know that something is wrong"
"Yes".

"And you also know that if I leave Dakota then everything I have here, everything I am, will be gone - it will all be lost"

"Yes. Agreed. But what will you have gained Eddie - what would your new life look like?"

"I don't know Mike, I have no idea what a new life, a real life, would look like. All I've ever known is here. I've been here providing services for people for so long, it's like I've forgotten who I am".

"Then you have to remember Eddie, you have to leave - you can't wait for things to happen, for The Panel to send more Johansson's, you have to start afresh."

"And what would happen to this place, to you, and to Lorna? I couldn't leave you here, to fend for yourselves, I just couldn't".

"You couldn't leave a girl who lives from day to day and a hired hit man to fend for themselves Eddie? Really? Listen to yourself. Anyway, I have an idea".

" Hold on to that thought Mike, I need to speak to Greg".

I walked back over to Greg and offered him more coffee. He looked a little dishevelled for sure and now that Mike had mentioned it, maybe a bit in need of a shave.

"Another coffee Greg?" I asked him.

" Great. Thanks Eddie. Say, could I ask you something? "

"Sure, fire away"

"Lorna….. "

"What about Lorna?"

" Is she….? "

"Is she…..what Greg?"

"Is she seeing anyone, do you know? If she is that's fine, it's just she's …you know? "

"No?" I wasn't going to make this easy for him " …..no, I don't know? "

"Kinda nice…you know, genuine, real…you know?"

My first instinct was to show him a brief glimpse of my real self…you know? Just for a few seconds. My second instinct was to introduce him to my real self on a continued basis…say…just for a day or so...you know? I took a deep breath and calmed myself. Lorna was now a grown woman at least physically, and if I was going to leave then I wouldn't be around to look out for her every day….and she was a good-looking woman, she was bound to catch people's attention.

"I don't know Greg, let me ask her and come back to you?"

" Sure, thanks Eddie - that would be good if you could."

"No problem. Say Greg, whatever happened to you just staying a couple or three days? I thought you had things to sort, you know, places to be?"

" Hey ! sounds like you're trying to get rid of me ? "

"No. No. Not at all, it's just that if you are looking at leaving, and you're thinking of asking Lorna out…then….look, I'm just a bit protective of her that's all, no offence, she's had a tough time recently and I'd hate….. "

"Oh, yeh, sure - I understand Eddie…no…no offence meant… is she…?"

"I'll ask her. OK?"

" Thanks Eddie"

So, that's why he was still here was it? - He was sweet on our Lorna. I wondered if he would still be if he saw her now. Certainly, she was more his age now, but I couldn't see her going for it myself, but…each to their own. I'd ask her and let her decide.

"Mike? Gotta minute?"

" Yep, what's up? "

" Could you bring Mr Hanson to my office please - even if he doesn't want to?"

"My pleasure"

"Let him finish his coffee first though I'll see you there."

Chapter Twenty-Two

A short time later a slightly dishevelled Mr Hanson and a beaming Mike walked into my office, well, one walked, and one was dragged into my office.

"Ah. Mr Hanson, glad you could make it, please take a seat".

"Eddie….Mr….? What's going on…what sort of place is this….? What have I done?" He stammered, as he was placed lightly but firmly in the chair near my desk.

" Explain this" I said as I threw the object at him.

"It's a mirror…?"

" I know it's a mirror. .. "

"It's for looking into…?"

" I know what it's for…"

"Then…..?"

" What are you doing with it? "

"At the moment, nothing Eddie…I couldn't find it this morning, I normally use it for ….look, it's a shaving mirror, it says so on the back….look if you don't believe me."

"I know it's a shaving mirror Mr Johansson."

"Hanson"

"What…?"

" Hanson….my name is Hanson…. James Oliver Hanson, but everyone calls me Greg…Greg Hanson….what's all this about? Please Eddie? What do you think I have done? "

"Ah…." said Mike from the side of the man in front of me.

" Ah? " I said.

"Yeah, Eddie….um….he's right….I must have read the card wrong…" Mike explained as he turned it over in his hands.

" What? "

"Look….look at the card…please" said the soon to be correct Mr J O Hanson.

I took the card from Mike and looked at it.

"Ah" I said, but then thought "what about this?" and passed him the second mirror " What is that for then? "

"Possibly…..and there is no sarcasm intended here at all….is it also for looking into?" Greg suggested.

" Yes. But why was it taped to the underneath of your bedside cabinet? "

"Your bedside cabinet Eddie surely? Well, one of your bedside cabinets"

"Yes. Technically speaking, but in your room….and if you say….'your room' there will be problems. Have you seen it before? Why was it there?"

" No. And I have no idea. Look, I'll just leave, I won't say anything I promise, there's obviously been some mistake, you've got me mixed up with someone else….I'll just go… and we 'll forget this ever happened? What do you say? "

"Yes. That seems like the best idea Mr Hanson. I can only sincerely apologise for

279

the misunderstanding. Obviously there will be no charge for your stay - and can I offer you anything for your journey? A flask of coffee? A sandwich of some sort? Do you have a long way to go ?"

"Eddie?" Mike asked, but I ignored him.

"That's very kind Eddie, thank you but no, I will be on my way if it's all the same to you? " Greg assured me.

"Understood. Again, on behalf of Eddie's Diner, and me personally, I do apologise for any inconvenience caused and wish you a safe and pleasant onward journey. Mike, could I ask you to accompany Mr Hanson to his vehicle?"

" Sure Eddie. Hey Mr Johansson? No hard feelings? " I looked at Mike as he spoke.

"Absolutely, purely a misunderstanding" Greg said.

I nodded to Mike and the pair of them left the office.

It was the following day - I was in the kitchen, my favourite place and the music was on. I'd set up the Rock Ola with a few uplifting songs at full volume. Whilst I'd definitely selected them myself, she had had other ideas and I had to listen to Destiny's Child - Survivor, before getting to The Man - Eminem - Lose Yourself, followed by Not Afraid. I was just singing loud and off key to The Boss - Born to Run, when the door opened, and Mike walked in. He looked dusty and a little tired I have to say.

" Great song, but you're The Boss Eddie, not Springsteen. How did you know? "
"You called him Johansson and he didn't flinch…not even a bit."
" Yeah. Amateur. Any chance of a Dakota Special? "
"Sure. On the house. Where did you go? "
"Eventually…?"
" Rock Falls" we said together.

We turned the music down a shade so we could speak, and Mike sat at the counter to eat. He'd had a long couple of days and as I poured him coffee he asked.

"Was it just that?"

" No. I thought I'd seen him before, but I couldn't think where, and then it came to me. When I had that meeting?"

"The outta town one?"

"The outta town one - he walked past - just in the background, just for a moment, but it was there, in my mind - it had been bothering me, but it was him being smug, even then, in that chair, in my office - it annoyed me, and it jogged a memory - that's when I knew".

"Arrogance. Is he one of The Panel then?"

"No. I think he was just a lackey - just someone they sent - a no-one really".

"Well, he is now - he's at the bottom of a cliff in Rock Falls with all the other Johansson's".

"Another coffee Mike?"

"Sure. Why not"

"We need to plan. We need to think how we can deal with this now - they will be coming. When they don't get a report from Greg, they will come".

"And when they come Eddie, you need to be gone. You can't stay here. They will reassign you…or worse".

"No. I need to be here, but subservient, compliant, at least for the time being. Time will sort itself out in Dakota, with or without me I've decided. The Panel doesn't need me, specifically me, to do their bidding - I'm just a pencil pusher when it comes to it. Once you get to know the rules and regs it's just filling in forms really, sending returns that sort of thing. Experience counts sure, but that comes with time, if you see what I mean and I have had plenty of that, but just none for myself".

"And do you have a plan Eddie?"

"I have but I need to speak to Lorna first - I need to make sure she's OK and that she's going to be OK".

I then told Mike my plan and, whilst he wasn't happy with it at first, he saw how it made sense - for me, for him. And for Lorna it wouldn't make any difference at all if she still wanted what she said she wanted.
I knocked on Lorna's door and she told me to come in.

"Hi Lorna. Are you OK" I asked her
"Sure Eddie. What's up?" she asked me.
"Nothing. Everything. But nothing that you need to worry about. I need to speak to you. I need to be honest with you"
"Again? How honest can one person be Eddie?"
"Never enough Lorna. Never too honest. Look. Mike needs to go away".
"Oh? A business meeting?"

"Kinda. Yeah. But a long one, and while he's gone you and I will be in charge. Do you think that would be good - you and I in charge of everything?

"Sure Eddie - kinda management now am I?"

"Yeah. Why not? You've been here a while now - you deserve a pay rise, and hey, why not a new title - how about Assistant Manager? How does that sound?"

"The pay rise sounded better Eddie to be honest, but I'll take the title as well - do I get a badge?"

"Sure. I'll sort you a badge to go with the new job. There's a lot more responsibility though - you ready for that?"

"Oh yes. No problems Eddie - I can handle it".

"The only thing is Lorna; you won't be able to just stay here. You'd have to go out - get stuff - supplies and so on".

"OK…?"

"You'd have to, what's the word….'mix'
with people"

"OK…?"

"Which means you would have to …
you know…?"

"No. Eddie….what?"

"Well, sort of manage…you'd have to
actually deal with people, not just in the
diner - you ready for that?"

"Would I still have a tips jar though?"

"Well - the waitresses would - but you'd
manage it - you know, deal with
stuff overall"

"OK. Which means I'd have to be here -
actually be here, day to day…and
not…like I wanted"

"Oh. Thank God for that Lorna. You
worried me. No. Not like you wanted. You
will need to be here, actually be here, to
help me, to run the place if I'm not about.
Think you will be able to do that?"

"Sure. I'm older now, I feel older anyway,
more…what's the word?"

"Mature?"

"Yeah. Mature - now that's an old word. By the way…where's Mike going?"

"He doesn't know yet. He hasn't got that far in his plan just yet. But he'll get there I'm sure."

Chapter Twenty-Three

I think Weary Traveller, you are way ahead of me, and you have already guessed what happened back then, what had to happen. Mike and I changed places. Was it that obvious? Could I have done anything else? But did I really have any   other choice?

Mike was happy with it - it was partly his decision, his choice to make as well as mine. He said I wasn't that bad looking really, and bearing in mind his appearance won't change in centuries, I think he's got a good deal overall. I hope he manages to convince The Panel that he's me - he's certainly been around long enough to know the rules and regs, and - the rest? Well, that's just all facade really - doing and saying the right things at the right times and keeping your head down.

Lorna will be happy I'm sure in her new role as Assistant Manager - she's got a badge and a pay rise, and I know Mike will look out for her - I know he'll keep her away from fast cars and fast men. I'm sure she'll grow into her new life and remember each and every day as she dishes out the tips for her new staff - I understand the place has grown a lot since I left - there was a new road built which brought a lot of traffic the diner's way - so that will keep her busy, keep her occupied.

I could have stayed. I could have argued my case with The Panel, but you know what they were like. It wouldn't have mattered what I'd said to them - they wouldn't have listened - like a lot of management really. Oh, they would have nodded and 'uh hu'd' in all the right places, but at the end of any meeting they would have just said 'we'll let you know'. But they wouldn't have - I would have been reassigned…or worse.

So, Me? Well, I know I have about a year to live - that's what Mike had on his original plan, and now that I'm abroad - I won't tell you where, as it might cause you problems, but I am enjoying that year. I'm a lot older than he used to be - they say that age does eventually catch up with you, but boy, this was a bit quicker than I thought it was going to be. It's strange, when I left Dakota I was forty-seven - not a bad age for a would-be retired hit man and I have to say, Mike was not an unfit man, but now, about a year later I am starting to creak.

It's a strange sensation getting old - yes, I know time wise I am centuries old, but Mike's body …well let's just say that seventy-seven came on all of a sudden, and it's been a bit of a shock.

I'm happy that I've been to the places I have in the past year. I've travelled near and far, east, and west - I'm so glad that Mike's passport had a few years left on it - good old Mike Flanagan. I've seen the pyramids, I've seen the Taj Mahal, I've seen The Great Wall of China. I've visited a lot of the sights that 'they' say you have to see. Looking back, Dakota was such a small place when I was there. I remember it fondly obviously - it was my home for hundreds of years - but the world is so much bigger than just one state - it has so much to offer, and I know that I won't get to see everything, as I would have if I had had Time on my side. But even if I did, unlike you I don't think I would ever be weary of it - but now I will never know.

I asked you at the beginning of my tale - what would you give to live someone else's life, for a year, a month, or even a day? Would you give everything, for just that chance? And I know that my choice was brought on me by circumstances. Would I have swapped everything with Mike if I didn't have to? Probably not. I probably wouldn't have given it another thought if things hadn't changed - I would have had no need to make any choice at all. I probably would have continued for all eternity.

But I *have* however given up eternity for just one year - a chance to see what I could in a brief, oh so brief period of time.

I could have stayed and lived as I had done for hundreds of years and never thought any differently. But circumstances changed and made me think outside my situation. Made me lift my head up. Made me decide, an uncomfortable decision, but, in my humble opinion, based only on my experience the correct decision for me, and it is all about choice.

So here I am in….well, let's just say in Europe, in the sun, enjoying a latte and not really thinking of anything in particular. I sit with my face, well Mike's face, pointing upwards and talking to you, looking back on my time.

A woman walks past, and I look at *her* face - she seems familiar somehow.

She walks a few more steps, then she stops and turns around.

"Hello?" she says, a curious look on that pretty face.

"Hello madam? Can I help you" always the helper

"Do I know you?" she asks.

"I don't think so. Are you local?"

"From here? No. I am not local - and by your accent, neither are you. You're American, right?"

"Yes. Originally - as original as an American could be" I forget myself just for a brief moment.

"I thought so, but with a hint of….Scottish? Irish perhaps?"

"Oh, yes. Irish. Michael. My name is Michael".

"No, it isn't….Etu" she says, as two other people appear from nowhere and sit at my table. "You need to come home. Oh, and by the way my name is Greta…. Johansson, obviously."

Printed in Great Britain
by Amazon